# THE BROKEN RED CORD

THARUN K

*To the lovers who, despite heartbreak and the distance, are still fighting hard to rebuild the love once they lost.*

# Contents


*About Author*     *vii*

*Foreword*     *ix*

*Preface*     *xi*

*Acknowledgements*     *xiii*

*Prologue*     *xv*

1. When Love First Bloomed...     1

2. When We Met...     28

3. When Distance Grew...     57

4. The RED Cord...     83

5. Keeping The Flame Alive...     105

6. Shattered Thread...     140

7. The Shadow Of Her Light...     157

# About Author

Tharun k

Tharun born on April 11, 2003. In Thirthahalli, a town in Shivamogga district. Having spent most of his time in hometown. Now currently residing in Bengaluru. He has also written his first book *Rebloomed Love*, In 2024.

You can reach him at,

Instagram - @tharun_scribes @ _tharun._.k

Email – tharunpartha23@gmail.com.

# Foreword

Love, in its most profound form, is a journey sometimes tender, sometimes turbulent, but always transformative. This story begins with a boy whose heart beats only for one person, the girl who becomes the centre of his world. His devotion knows no bounds as he relentlessly pursues her, facing challenges, doubts, and his own insecurities. Through perseverance and sincerity, he finally wins her heart, achieving the dream he thought would make him whole.

Yet, as with many love stories, their union is only the beginning. Relationships are built on trust and understanding, delicate threads that must be nurtured with care. A small misunderstanding trivial to some but monumental to them threatens to unravel the bond they fought so hard to create. The boy learns a hard truth: love isn't just about winning someone's heart; it's about keeping it through storms of doubt.

This tale explores the raw and often messy complexities of love, reminding us that no matter how strong a connection may seem, it requires effort, patience, and forgiveness to endure. It is a story of longing, joy, and heartbreak, but most importantly, it is a story of growth.

As you journey through these pages, you may find echoes of your own experiences or lessons to take into your own relationships. Enjoy the journey, and may you come to understand love not just as a destination, but as a lifelong adventure.

# Preface

Love is a journey of triumph and tenderness, but it is also fraught with challenges that test its strength. This story follows a boy who pours his heart into winning the love of his life, overcoming every obstacle to make her his. Their love blossoms into something beautiful, but a small misunderstanding, a moment of doubt threatens to unravel everything they built together.

Through joy and heartbreak, this tale explores the fragility of love and the lessons hidden in loss. It's a reminder that even in love's most painful moments, there lies a chance for growth and redemption

# Acknowledgements

Writing *The Broken Red Cord* has been an emotional journey, and I owe my deepest gratitude to everyone who inspired and supported me along the way. To my readers, thank you for embracing stories of love, heartbreak, and resilience.

To my friends and family, your unwavering belief in me gave me the courage to bring this story to life.

I'd like to extend my deepest gratitude to the brave souls who helped me bring this book to life. You've earned a special place in my acknowledgements.

Your guidance and feedback were invaluable – without them, this book would probably be twice as long and three times as confusing.

A huge round of applause for Ananya, my proofreading superhero. She fearlessly tackled my manuscript, slaying typos and grammatical errors with the precision of a seasoned warrior. I'm pretty sure she deserves a medal (and possibly hazard pay).

And a massive thank you to my amazing friends, who, fueled by endless cups of tea at our adda, somehow managed to convince me that I could actually write a book. You're either incredibly supportive or incredibly gullible. Either way, thank you!

While they say you shouldn't judge a book by its cover, a compelling cover is undeniably important for a book's aesthetic appeal. I'm deeply grateful to myself for my talent and hard work in creating such a striking and effective cover. My contribution has truly elevated the book's presentation. Thank you, myself.

Lastly, to those who have experienced the pain of separation and the beauty of healing, this story is for you.

May it remind us all that even broken cords can teach us the strength to mend.

The title of the story is inspired by a Japanese mythical story of a red cord. It is said that two soulmates will be ties by a red thread by gods. The thread may tangle but will never break. It will always find its way back.

# Prologue

The air was heavy it was a cold winter morning he was holding his phone and sitting on his bed. This was where it had all begun where he had saw her profile, where he had decided that she was the one who could fill the empty spaces in his heart.

For years, he had poured every ounce of himself into winning her over. Every glance, every smile, every shared moment had been a small victory, a step closer to the love he had craved. But love, as he would come to learn, is not just about getting; it's about keeping. Their love story had been beautiful, passionate, and fragile. Like a castle built on sand, it had seemed unshakable until the tide of misunderstanding washed it away.

Now, he sat alone, the echoes of her laughter haunting the quiet night. The boy who once believed that love could conquer anything now grappled with a new question:

*What do you do when love slips through your fingers, and you're left holding only memories?*

This is the story of a boy who fought for love, lost it, and learned the hardest lesson of all—that sometimes, love isn't enough, but sometimes, it's worth fighting for again.

# 1

## When Love First Bloomed...

It was a cold winter morning, and I was just waking up. As I reached for my phone, I noticed seven unread messages from the same contact. I couldn't bring myself to open them, I already knew what they were about, and fear gripped me. I had always been afraid. Afraid of the choices I made, afraid of the consequences, afraid of life itself.

But for the past four years, fear had taken a back seat. My life had been clear, my decisions steady. And the reason for that clarity was her Pari. She wasn't just someone I loved; she was my guiding light. With her beautiful face, cute smile, deep black eyes, and hair that was neither too curly nor too straight, Pari had become my anchor.

It all started when I was in the 7$^{th}$ std. one day as I was sitting in the desk casually talking to my friends the door opened, and in walked Pari, my classmate since Pre-KG. I had known her well, but that day, something was different.

She was wearing a purple and black kurthi, her hair loosely flowing around her face. The moment I saw her; I felt a strange flutter in my chest. It was as if the world had paused for a moment, and the cool breeze that swept through the room only made her seem even more ethereal. I couldn't explain it, but it was as if something deep inside him had awakened.

From that moment on, I began to see Pari in a different light. What had once been a simple friendship now felt like something more, something pure and beautiful. I didn't understand it, but I knew that I wanted to be with her.

Some might argue that me, being just a small boy, couldn't possibly understand love. But to me, love was something simple and pure. I didn't know anything about the complexities of relationships or societal expectations. All I knew was that I wanted to make her happy, spend time with her, and share everything with her. I was ready to face any consequence, no matter what for just to be by her side.

For weeks, I had been gathering the courage to finally confess my feelings to her. Every time I saw her, my heart would race, my words would falter, but deep inside, I knew I couldn't keep my emotions buried any longer. I had rehearsed my confession over and over again, imagining the moment she would hear the truth the moment my heart would finally be free.

But fate had other plans. On the very day I had decided to bare my soul to her, I received the news that shattered me completely. Her family was moving to another town. And just like that, before I even had the chance to tell her how much she meant to me, she was gone.

The weight of that loss was unbearable. My chest felt hollow, my hands trembled, and my mind kept replaying all the moments we had shared, now tainted with the ache of what could have been. To make it even more painful, that day wasn't just any other day. It was my birthday. The one day that was supposed to bring happiness had instead left me with an emptiness I couldn't put into words.

I stood there, wondering if she had any idea, if she would ever know what I never got the chance to say.

Years passed, and life moved forward, but some feelings never truly fade.

It had been two and a half years since that day, the day I lost my chance to tell her how I felt. I had convinced myself that time would heal everything, that I would eventually forget, that maybe what I felt was just a fleeting crush. But all those illusions shattered the moment I saw her again.

It was at an NCC camp, of all places. The instant my eyes landed on her, it was as if time rewound itself. Every suppressed emotion, every unsaid word, came rushing back with an intensity I wasn't prepared for. She looked the same yet different more mature, more graceful, but still the same girl who had unknowingly held my heart all these years.

But just like before, I couldn't bring myself to speak to her. She still lived in another city, still felt like someone just out of reach. So, I let the days pass in silence, stealing glances when I could, pretending she wasn't there when she absolutely was. Even though I had seen her on the first day, I chose to stay in the shadows, fearing that my voice would betray the storm of emotions within me.

Then, on the tenth and final day of the camp, she came to me.

"Why didn't you talk to me?" Pari asked, her voice laced with a mixture of confusion and something else something almost like hurt.

I had no answer. How could I possibly explain? How could I tell her that after two and a half years of missing her, longing for her, I still wasn't brave enough? That the fear of losing whatever fragile thread still connected us was greater than the urge to speak?

So, I forced a small smile and said the only thing that felt safe. "I thought you would've forgotten me by now."

She looked at me, her eyes searching mine, before she said something that made my heart ache in a way I didn't expect.

"How could I forget you? We've been friends since Pre-KG. I've known you for as long as I've known how to talk."

At that moment, I didn't know whether to feel relieved or shattered. Because even though she remembered me, I wondered if she had ever seen me the way I saw her.

That day, our conversation was left incomplete unfinished hanging in the air like a question without an answer.

I forced a small smile, the kind that hides more than it reveals, and simply said, "Bye, Pari."

She didn't stop me. She didn't ask anything more. And maybe that hurt the most . how easily we let that moment slip away when it was the one conversation that shouldn't have been left incomplete.

Some conversations are better when left unfinished, left to linger as memories rather than realities. But not this one. Not ours.

Yet, what choice did I have? I wasn't brave enough then, just as I hadn't been years ago. And so, I walked away, carrying the weight of unspoken words and a heart that still wasn't ready to let go.

**Fate had given me a third chance.**

It was during the lockdown, a time when the world had come to a standstill, yet somehow, destiny was still at work, weaving our paths together once more.

The next time I saw her wasn't in person, but on Instagram. It had been three years since the NCC camp, three years since I had last seen her. But even through a screen, she took my breath away. One glimpse was all it took one photo, one moment and everything I had buried deep inside me came rushing back like a flood.

I realized then how much I had always wanted her.

This time, things were different. We started talking again, and as days turned into weeks, we slowly found our way back to the friendship we had lost. With every conversation, every late-night chat, it felt as though time had never separated us. And before I even realized it, something beautiful was happening, she had started to like me too.

But fear is a strange thing. Even when everything seemed perfect, even when I knew she felt something for me, I couldn't bring myself to confess. I had lost her twice before, and I wasn't willing to risk losing her again, not when we had finally rebuilt what once felt broken. So, I kept my feelings locked away, convincing myself that this was enough.

Then one day, out of nowhere, she gathered the courage that I never could.

Over a call, with a voice both nervous and determined, Pari spoke.

"Can I tell you something?" she asked, her voice softer than usual.

"Of course," I said, though my heart had already begun to race.

She hesitated for a moment, then took a deep breath.

"I don't know when it happened exactly, but for the past two or three months, I've started liking you... more than just a friend," she admitted, her voice barely above a whisper. "And I don't know if it makes any sense, but I couldn't keep it in anymore."

I felt my chest tighten, my mind struggling to process the words I had waited years to hear. My silence stretched too long, and she let out a nervous laugh.

"You're not saying anything... does that mean I ruined everything?" she asked hesitantly.

I closed my eyes, took a shaky breath, and finally, after all these years, I let my heart speak.

"Pari... I've loved you for as long as I can remember. I was just too much of a coward to say it."

Silence. Then, a soft laugh, filled with relief, joy, and something deeper.

"Took you long enough," she said, and I could almost see the smile in her voice.

And just like that, everything changed.

I still remember the exact moment it all began: August 23, 2021, at 2:03 a.m. That was when she confessed that she had feelings for me. It felt surreal. The girl I had loved since the seventh grade was finally mine. All the waiting, all the quiet longing, it was worth it.

Pari wasn't just beautiful; she had a heart as pure as her smile. Her innocence, her kindness, the way her chubby cheeks glowed when she laughed everything about her felt like a dream. Her voice didn't just reach my ears; it touched my soul. I could have spent a lifetime just listening to her talk.

Our relationship started as a long-distance one. Though we had been classmates in primary school and met briefly at the NCC camp, we hadn't seen each other in person since then. Even as we grew closer, we hadn't video-called yet. So, when we finally confessed our feelings, we decided to FaceTime the next day.

I was ecstatic. I couldn't wait to see her eyes looking back at me as we talked. Technology might not replace real eye contact, but it was the best we could do during the lockdown. That night, sleep evaded me. I was too excited, too restless, imagining what it would be like to see her face again.

The next morning felt like a milestone. For the first time, we would talk face-to-face, even if it was through a screen. It was a huge step for us because our love wasn't based on appearances it was rooted in who we were. Still, I couldn't deny how beautiful she was, as stunning as a rose in full bloom

I had been ardently waiting for her call all night, my eyes flickering to the clock as I paced restlessly around the room. The anticipation was unbearable. Finally, at around 10:30, it dawned on me, I needed to shower, wash my face, and make myself presentable. After all, she was going to see me after so long, and I had been out in the sun far too much lately, my skin now bearing a deep tan.

Time was slipping away, and I only had thirty minutes to get ready. I rushed to the bathroom, letting the cool water wash away my nerves, and emerged feeling somewhat refreshed. By the time I stepped back into the room, it was already 10:55. Hastily, I got dressed, grabbed my phone, and sat on the edge of the bed, clutching it tightly.

Then, at precisely 11:00, the phone rang exactly on time, not a second too early or late. It was as if the universe itself had synchronized for this moment.

I picked up the call, and the moment her face appeared on the screen, I was utterly captivated. Her mesmerizing eyes and radiant smile greeted me, stealing my breath away. I couldn't help but stare, completely entranced. Words escaped me; my mind went blank, leaving me in a stunned silence.

Sensing my speechlessness, Pari broke the quiet with a soft, "Hi," her voice as melodic and angelic as I had remembered.

I finally managed to reply, "Hello," breaking the awkward silence that had lingered at the start of the call. My delayed response had already made things uncomfortable, and I needed to ease into the conversation.

"You look fresh," Pari remarked, her eyes sparkling with curiosity.

"Yeah, I just showered a few minutes ago," I replied with a faint smile.

"I noticed your hair's still wet," she said with a playful grin.

Seizing the moment, I asked, "Why didn't you text me this morning? I was waiting."

Pari's smile deepened as she explained, "I was waiting for a video call. If I had texted you in the morning, we'd have ended up finishing half our conversation over text."

Her words hit me like a revelation. It wasn't the universe synchronizing for this moment; it was Pari, patiently waiting to call, creating this perfect timing all on her own.

I was overjoyed to see that Pari was just as excited to talk to me as I was to talk to her. But as we conversed, something felt off. It wasn't like the old days when our conversations flowed effortlessly. We were both holding back, not quite opening up the way we used to.

We kept avoiding eye contact, both of us looking away from the screen, as if the mere act of meeting each other's gaze would reveal too much. It was as if we were still processing the fact that we had just confessed our feelings over text the day before.

Talking to someone over text is one thing it's easy to hide behind words, to keep a certain distance. But a video call?

That was different. It was a whole new level of intimacy, and it felt like we were both still adjusting to the reality of it.

I needed something to break the ice between us, something we could both talk about comfortably. The silence between us was thick, and the awkwardness was palpable. We were both too shy to admit that we were, in a way, in a relationship. The words felt heavy, too real, and neither of us was ready to fully embrace that reality just yet.

I searched for a topic, something light and familiar, that could ease the tension and help us feel like ourselves again. But every time I opened my mouth, the words felt too big, too loaded. I knew we needed to find our rhythm again, but for now, we were stuck in this strange limbo, caught between what we had been and what we were becoming

Then, as I sat there, racking my brain for something, anything to say, a sudden thought popped into my mind. Oreo. My new dog. Pari absolutely adored her. She had seen Oreo in the photos I'd sent her before, and maybe in one or two short videos where Oreo was clumsily chasing her own tail or playfully jumping around. Pari had always gushed over how cute she was, how fluffy her little ears looked, and how adorable her curious eyes were. But she had never seen Oreo live. She hadn't witnessed how playful and mischievous she could be, especially when she was around me.

A smile crept onto my face. This was it. This would break the ice. I knew it. Oreo was something simple, something warm, and something that would bring out Pari's joy, her unfiltered excitement. It was the perfect way to pull us out of the shy, awkward silence we had found ourselves in.

I took a deep breath, trying to sound casual as I asked, *"Do you want to see Oreo?"*

For a split second, there was silence on the other end, and then her reply came through, brimming with excitement.

*"Yes! For sure!"*

Her words practically bounced off the screen with joy. I could picture her eyes lighting up and her face breaking into that wide, beautiful smile of hers. I grinned to myself, relieved and happy that I'd struck the right chord.

*"Okay, wait a second,"* I replied, getting up from my bed. Oreo was curled up in her favourite spot near the window, her tiny chest rising and falling as she napped peacefully. "Oreo, come here, girl," I called softly, crouching down. Her ears perked up at the sound of my voice, and within seconds, she was bounding toward me, her little paws tapping excitedly against the floor.

I couldn't help but laugh as she jumped up, wagging her tail like crazy, already ready to play. *"Good girl,"* I murmured, scratching behind her ears.

Pari's face was appearing on the screen, glowing with anticipation. "Where's Oreo? Show me!" she demanded playfully, her voice bubbling with excitement.

"Hold on, hold on," I said, laughing as I turned the camera toward Oreo, who was now trying to nuzzle my hand, clearly thrilled at all the attention. "Here she is!"

The moment Oreo's fluffy little face popped up on the screen, Pari let out a delighted squeal. "Oh my God, look at her! She's so adorable!" Her voice was a mix of awe and pure joy, and I could see her face light up completely.

"Oreo, say hi to Pari," I teased, holding the phone closer to Oreo. Oreo tilted her head at the sound of Pari's voice, her ears flopping to the side in that curious way that always made me laugh.

"She's looking at me! Oh my God, she's looking at me!" Pari exclaimed, her laughter echoing through the call. "She's so cute, I can't handle this!"

I couldn't stop smiling as I watched Oreo's antics. She started chasing after my hand, thinking it was a game, and Pari burst into laughter again. "She's so playful! I want to hug her!"

"Yeah, she's a little ball of energy," I said, grinning as Oreo tried to climb onto my lap, her tail wagging furiously. "She's always like this,never sits still."

Pari's laughter softened into a warm smile. "You're so lucky to have her. She's like a little ray of sunshine."

I paused for a moment, looking at Oreo as she snuggled against me, and then back at Pari on the screen. "Yeah," I said softly, "she really is."

For a while, we just talked about Oreo, about her favourite foods, her silly habits, and how much Pari wanted to meet her in person. The conversation flowed so naturally that I almost forgot how awkward things had felt just minutes ago. Oreo had done exactly what I hoped she would. She had brought us back to the easy, comfortable rhythm we'd always shared.

At one point, Pari said with a teasing smile, "You know, I think Oreo likes me more than you."

"Oh, really?" I replied, raising an eyebrow. "She's my dog, remember?"

Pari laughed. "Doesn't matter. I'm claiming her as mine when I visit."

I shook my head, pretending to be exasperated, but I couldn't hide my grin. "Fine. But she's only yours for a day. After that, she's mine again."

"Deal," Pari said, her smile softening. "But seriously, thank you for showing her to me. I really needed this."

I looked at her then, at the way her face glowed with happiness, and realized how much this little moment had meant to both of us. It wasn't just about Oreo. It was about us, about finding a way back to the comfort and laughter we'd always shared.

"Anytime," I said quietly, my voice sincere.

And as Oreo curled up beside me, Pari still laughing and talking on the screen, I knew one thing for certain: this was just the beginning. The ice between us had melted, and in its place was something real, something warm, and something I didn't want to let go of.

After talking about Oreo, we both felt more comfortable. The awkward silence from earlier had vanished, replaced by laughter, playful teasing, and the easy flow of conversation that had always defined us. Yet, despite the comfort we now shared, saying those three words '*I love you*' still felt a little too big for the moment. It wasn't that I didn't want to say it. I did. But it was only our second day since we had admitted we liked each other, and the weight of those words hung in the air like something precious yet fragile.

I couldn't bring myself to say it out loud, especially not over a video call. Somehow, it felt too raw, too direct, and maybe even too soon. So, I decided I would text her later, once we finished our call. That way, I could say what I felt without the added pressure of seeing her reaction in real time.

We continued talking casually for another twenty minutes. The conversation was light about college, some random funny incidents, and how Oreo had completely stolen her heart. She laughed easily, and I found myself smiling at her every expression. She had a way of making even the smallest things feel special.

Eventually, she glanced at the clock and said, "I have some work to do. I'll call you later, okay?"

"Sure," I replied, trying to sound casual, though my heart had already started pounding. This was it,the moment I had been preparing for in my head. I smiled at her through the screen, trying to keep it cool.

"Bye, idiot," she said playfully, giving me a small wave.

"Bye, Pari," I replied, my voice steady.

And with that, the call ended.

I stared at the blank screen for a moment, taking a deep breath. *Okay, now's the time,* I thought. My plan was simple: if she had told me "I love you" first, I would have said it back instantly. But since she hadn't, I would take the first step now. I didn't want to leave those words unsaid any longer.

I opened our chat, my fingers hovering over the keyboard. The screen felt too bright, and the words I wanted to type felt heavier than they should have. Finally, I typed:

**"Love you."**

I stared at the message for a few seconds, my thumb hesitating over the send button. My heart raced like it was about to burst out of my chest. It was ridiculous how nervous I felt, considering we had already admitted we liked each other. But this, this felt different.

Finally, I hit send.

The message disappeared into the chat, and the familiar double tick appeared, showing it had been delivered. Now came the hardest part: waiting. My phone screen remained silent for what felt like an eternity, though it was probably just a few seconds. I kept staring at it, my mind running wild with a million thoughts. *What if she doesn't reply? What if she's shocked?*

And then, the screen lit up. A notification.

Pari is typing...

My heart skipped a beat. I held my breath, watching those three little dots blink on the screen.

Finally, her reply came through:

**"Love you too, idiot. ♥?"**

I exhaled, a mix of relief and joy flooding through me. A smile spread across my face one I couldn't hide even if I tried. I read her message twice, maybe three times, just to let it sink in.

That simple reply made everything feel real. She loved me too. It wasn't just in my head, and it wasn't just a fleeting moment. It was real, and it was ours.

I flopped back onto my bed, my heart still racing but in the best way possible. I stared at her message, the little heart emoji making me smile even more. *Love you too, idiot.* That was so her,playful, sweet, and completely perfect.

And just like that, all the awkwardness, all the hesitation, melted away. We had said it. The words were out there now, and there was no turning back.

It was a small moment, but it was everything.

Now that she had told me she loved me too, I felt a surge of confidence. The awkwardness that had plagued our first video call started to fade, and making eye contact while talking no longer felt like such a challenge. Our conversations became more natural, more comfortable, and undeniably more special.

Before I knew it, video calls became a part of our daily routine. We would talk for two hours on video, then switch to voice calls for another two hours, and in between, we'd text each other endlessly. Honestly, I lost track of how much time we spent chatting. It felt like my phone had become an extension of my hand, and my power bank was now my most trusted companion, always fully charged and ready to keep our conversations alive.

It wasn't just the quantity of our talks that amazed me, it was the quality. We talked about everything and nothing. From silly jokes to our dreams for the future, from teasing each other to moments of deep vulnerability, every conversation felt like it brought us closer. Even the sound of her laughter was enough to brighten my day.

Of course, my parents noticed the sudden spike in my phone usage. They weren't exactly thrilled about it.

"Why are you always on that phone? Can't you put it down for a while?" my mom would ask, her tone a mix of curiosity and irritation.

They warned me, scolded me, and even tried to impose time limits on my phone usage. But I was in love, and their words didn't faze me. How could they understand what it felt like to be so connected to someone, to feel like every second spent talking to her was a second well spent?

But I didn't care. Pari was worth every scolding, every suspicious glance, and every warning about my "unhealthy" phone habits. For the first time in my life, I felt like I was exactly where I was meant to be with her, even if it was just through a screen.

Love had a way of making everything else fade into the background. Time didn't matter, scoldings didn't matter, even sleep didn't matter. All that mattered was Her, her voice, her laughter, her presence. And in those moments, I felt like the happiest person in the world.

Despite everything, I still couldn't bring myself to say "I love you" directly during a video call or even over the phone. Even after Pari had texted that she loved me too, I felt shy and hesitant to confess it aloud. Instead, I relied on texts to express my feelings, thinking it was easier that way. But deep down, I knew it wasn't enough.

One day, as we were texting, she suddenly asked, *"Why don't you tell me 'I love you' directly? You just send it in a text after our calls."*

Her question caught me completely off guard. My fingers froze over the keyboard as I tried to come up with a response. I felt cornered, unsure of what to say. So, in a moment of deflection, I typed back, *"Why don't you tell me first? You do the same thing,you only say it over texts too."*

I thought that would buy me some time, but before I could even process what I had sent, my phone started ringing. It was her. My heart began pounding in my chest, each beat louder than the last. My palms grew clammy as I stared at her name flashing on the screen. What was she going to say?

With a deep breath, I picked up the call, trying to steady my voice.

Before I could even say hello, I heard her voice, soft and sweet, like the first drops of rain on a summer day. *"I love you, idiot,"* she said, her tone playful yet sincere.

I froze. It was the first time I had heard those words from her lips, spoken aloud, in her beautiful, angelic voice. It wasn't just the words it was the way she said them, with a mix of affection, teasing, and a hint of shyness.

My heart felt like it might burst from happiness. I couldn't help but smile, my cheeks warming as her words echoed in my ears. For a moment, I couldn't even speak.

"Are you there, or did you faint?" she teased, giggling softly.

"I... I'm here," I finally managed to say, my voice barely above a whisper.

Hearing her say those three words directly made me feel something I couldn't put into words. It wasn't just love,it was a kind of joy and completeness I had never felt before.

That moment changed everything. It gave me the courage I didn't know I had.

Now it was my turn to reply to her "I love you." I already had a bit of courage because she had said it first, but my nerves were still all over the place. I took a deep breath, gathered every ounce of bravery I could muster, and said, *"I love to you."*

Yes, I messed it up. Four simple words, and I completely fumbled.

For a moment, there was silence, and then Pari burst out laughing. Her laughter was so loud and contagious that I couldn't help but smile, even as I cringed at my blunder.

*"I know your love to me,"* she teased between giggles. *"But it's 'love you too,' silly."*

I felt my cheeks flush with embarrassment, but her laughter made it hard to stay self-conscious. We both ended up laughing together, the awkwardness melting away.

Trying to save face, I said, *"That's my unique way of saying 'love you too.'"*

*"Unique?!"* Pari replied, still laughing. *"It's not unique,it's weird! It gives a completely different meaning, you idiot!"*

Her playful scolding only made me laugh harder. In that moment, I realized something important: it didn't matter how clumsy or imperfect I was around her. Pari didn't care. She loved me for who I was, even when I stumbled over my words.

*"Fine, fine,"* I said, finally composing myself. *"Love you too, Pari."*

*"Now that's better,"* she replied, her voice softening, though I could still hear the smile in her tone.

That moment, despite its silliness, felt special. It wasn't perfect, but it was *us*. And I wouldn't trade it for anything in the world.

We were really hitting it off. It felt like we matched each other's vibe perfectly, as if we were two pieces of the same puzzle finally coming together. The more we talked, the stronger our bond grew. I found myself falling even deeper in love with her silly, playful talks, her angelic voice, and that radiant smile of hers. She was always on my mind, no matter what I was doing.

Even when I was playing with Oreo, my mischievous little dog, I'd catch myself thinking of Pari. Whenever Oreo did something naughty like chewing on my shoes or knocking over a cup,I'd instinctively say, *"Stop it, Pari maa! Don't do that!"* instead of scolding Oreo by name.

The first time it happened, I froze for a second, realizing my slip. It was both embarrassing and funny. Oreo tilted her head at me as if to say, *"Who's Pari maa?"* I couldn't help but laugh at myself. Pari had become such a constant presence in my thoughts that even my dog was starting to feel her influence.

When I told Pari about this little mix-up, she laughed so hard that I thought she might fall off her chair. *"Pari maa?!"* she exclaimed between giggles. *"Wow, I've officially replaced your dog in your heart!"*

*"Not just my heart, Pari maa,"* I teased. *"You've taken over my whole life!"*

*"Good,"* she replied playfully. *"Because I'm not going anywhere."*

And just like that, our silly banter turned into another memory I'd cherish forever. It was these little moments, the laughter, and the lightness, that made me realize how deeply I loved her.

We used to start silly fights just to spice things up, turning even the smallest things into playful drama. One of our favourite games was pretending to be characters from our old school days. Pari would take on the role of a strict, scary teacher, and I'd play the mischievous student who never did his homework.

Every time she asked me for my homework, I'd come up with the most ridiculous excuses. *"Ma'am, the dog ate it,"* I'd say, or *"I left it in my imaginary locker."* She would immediately get into character, scolding me in her sternest voice.

*"Partha, how many times have I told you to submit your homework on time? This is unacceptable!"* she'd say, her tone dripping with mock authority.

After her tirade, I'd start pretending to cry dramatically. *"You scolded me, Pari maa,"* I'd whine, exaggerating my voice like a melodramatic actor. *"I was just playing a student, but you scolded me because I'm Partha. Admit it,you're not mad at the student; you're mad at me!"*

She'd burst into laughter every single time, breaking character instantly. *"You're such a drama king!"* she'd say, still laughing. *"How can I be mad at you when you're this ridiculous?"*

But I wouldn't stop. *"No, Pari maa, I know the truth. You were angry at me, not the student!"*

She'd shake her head, trying to sound serious but failing miserably. *"Okay, fine! Maybe I was mad because you're impossible to deal with!"*

*"See? I knew it!"* I'd declare triumphantly, only to have her throw a pillow at the camera in mock frustration.

These playful moments made us feel closer, as if we were kids again, reliving the carefree days of our school lives but with a love that was now much deeper. It wasn't just about the laughter; it was about how comfortable we were with each other, how we could be completely ourselves without any filters. And in those moments, I realized that loving

Pari wasn't just about the big, romantic gestures,it was also about the silly fights, the playful banter, and the endless laughter that made every day with her feel like an adventure.

After that, I made it a habit to start little fights every time she called me "idiot" when she said "I love you." In response, I began calling her "Maa." It wasn't just a nickname,it was my playful way of showing how much I adored her. While "Maa" sounded sweet and endearing, she stuck to calling me "idiot," and I couldn't help but take it as both a term of endearment and a subtle jab at how ridiculous I often acted around her.

To be fair, she wasn't wrong. I did act like an idiot sometimes, especially when I was trying to make her laugh or tease her. But that didn't stop me from pretending to be offended. I'd pile up all her "idiots" in my imaginary complaint file, ready to throw them back at her in mock outrage.

*"You call me idiot every time! Why not something sweet, like love, darling, or Partha the Great?"* I'd whine dramatically.

She'd laugh, her voice dripping with mischief. *"Because you're my idiot, and no other nickname suits you better!"*

*"Oh, really? Well, in that case, you're Pari Maa. Because only a mother would tolerate such behaviour from her child!"* I'd reply with a smirk.

This playful banter became our thing. I'd start arguments over the silliest topics, not because I was actually upset, but because I loved the way she got flustered trying to defend herself.

*"Why do you keep calling me idiot? I'm keeping count, you know. That's the fifth time today!"* I'd tease her, pretending to take notes on a piece of paper.

*"You're impossible, Partha! What do you want me to call you? Genius? Einstein? Oh wait, how about Drama King?"* she'd fire back, unable to hide her laughter.

*"Drama King sounds good. But if you call me idiot one more time, I'm filing an official complaint!"* I'd declare, trying to sound serious but failing miserably.

*"File it wherever you want, idiot,"* she'd say with a wink, completely unfazed.

At the end of the day, I knew she called me "idiot" because she loved me, and I'd act like an idiot because I loved her too. These little fights weren't about winning or losing,they were about finding another excuse to talk, laugh, and stay connected. And as much as I pretended to be annoyed, I secretly loved every second of it.

It had been a month since we got committed, and I felt like it was time to do something special to make us even closer. I wanted to express everything I felt for Pari in a way that words over a call or text couldn't fully capture. That's when the idea struck me,I'd write her a letter. Something heartfelt and personal, something she could hold onto forever.

That night, I told Pari I was tired and needed to sleep early. *"Good night, Pari,"* I texted, adding a sleepy emoji for effect. She believed me, replying with a sweet, *"Good night, idiot. Sweet dreams!"*

But sleep was the last thing on my mind. As soon as I was sure she wasn't expecting any more messages, I grabbed a notebook and a pen. The room was dimly lit, with just my desk lamp glowing softly. Oreo was curled up at my feet, occasionally looking up at me as if she knew I was up to something important.

I stared at the blank page for a moment, trying to figure out how to start. Writing a letter felt so different from texting or calling. This wasn't just about saying "I love you"; it was about pouring my heart out in a way that would make her feel every bit of my emotions.

I started with something simple:

*"Dear Pari maa,*

The words started flowing naturally after that. I wrote about how much her smile meant to me, how her voice was the highlight of my day, and how she had this magical way of making even the most ordinary moments feel special. I told her how much I adored her playful scoldings, her calling me "idiot," and even the way she teased me relentlessly.

When I finished, I read it over a few times, making sure it was perfect. My handwriting was a bit messy in places, but I hoped that would make it feel more genuine.

The next morning, I woke up with excitement. I couldn't wait to tell her about the letter during our video call that evening. I knew she'd be surprised and, hopefully, touched by the gesture.

That night, as we started our usual call, I casually brought it up. *"Pari, I have something special for you."*

Her eyes lit up with curiosity. *"What is it? Tell me!"*

I smiled, holding up the letter. *"I wrote you something. A letter. I wanted to tell you how much you mean to me, and I thought this would be the best way."*

She was speechless for a moment, her cheeks turning a faint shade of pink. *"You really wrote me a letter? No one's ever done that for me before."*

I nodded, feeling a bit shy but also proud of myself. *"I'll read it to you if you want."*

*"Of course, I want to hear it!"* she said, her voice filled with excitement.

I took out the letter and started reading.

**Dear Pari maa,**

Happy one-month anniversary, my love! I never imagined that after all these years of being the crazy best friends that we are, I'd get to call you not just "Maa" but also my girlfriend,the girl I've loved secretly for so long.

You know, it's funny how life works. From the time we were just tiny kids in pre-KG, arguing over crayons and sharing snacks, to where we are now, it feels like the universe always had this beautiful plan for us. Do you remember those silly fights we'd have about who was smarter, or the times you'd call me an idiot for doing something ridiculous? Well, those little moments are etched in my heart because they remind me of *us*. The goofy, crazy, and imperfectly perfect *us*.

I still can't believe that I've loved you since I was a scrawny little 6th grader. Back then, I didn't have the courage to tell you how I felt. I was terrified that if I said anything, I'd lose the one person who meant the world to me. But here we are, all these years later, and not only did I not lose you, but I gained something even more beautiful,*your love.*

Every time you look at me with that twinkle in your eyes or call me "idiot" with that mischievous smile, my heart skips a beat. You might laugh at this (because you always do), but you've always been my dream, Pari. You're my first thought in the morning, my favourite memory of every day, and the one person who makes me believe in forever.

I love how we fight over the silliest things, only to end up laughing until our stomachs hurt. I love how you never fail to make me feel like the luckiest guy alive, even if it's by scolding me or making fun of me. You're my best friend, my anchor, and the one who makes everything in my world brighter.

These past 30 days have been nothing short of magical, but in my heart, it feels like I've loved you for a lifetime,because I have. It's not just this month, Maa. It's the 14 years of friendship, countless memories, and the way you've unknowingly held my heart since I was a kid.

Thank you for being mine, for letting me call you "Maa" even when you probably roll your eyes at it, and for loving this idiot of yours in your own beautiful way. I promise to keep annoying you, making you laugh, fighting with you, and loving you with all my heart for the rest of my life.

Here's to our first month together and to the many, many more months (and years) to come. I love you, Pari, more than words could ever say.

Yours forever,
**Your Idiot, Partha.**

As I read the letter to Pari, I noticed her eyes begin to glisten with unshed tears. The deeper I went into the words, the more emotional she became. Her expressions shifted from joy to tenderness, and then to something I couldn't quite describe,an overwhelming mix of love and vulnerability.

I, too, was feeling the weight of my emotions as I read. My voice wavered, and I had to pause a few times, taking deep breaths to steady myself and stop the lump in my throat from turning into full-blown tears. But Pari couldn't hold back. Her tears began to flow, rolling down her cheeks silently as she listened intently to every word.

When I finished reading, the room fell into a profound silence. I looked up at her, and for a moment, we just stared at each other. Her eyes were filled with love, glistening with the tears she couldn't stop, and my own were misty, threatening to spill over. Neither of us spoke right away, as if words would ruin the purity of the moment.

Finally, she broke the silence, her voice trembling with emotion. *"This... this is one of the best things I've ever heard in my life. If I were there with you right now, I'd hug you so tightly and cry until I was satisfied."*

Her words hit me like a wave, and I could feel my heart swell with both love and guilt. *"I'm sorry, Pari,"* I said softly. *"I didn't mean to make you cry."*

She shook her head quickly, a small, tearful smile forming on her lips. *"These aren't sad tears, you idiot. They're tears of joy and love. You have no idea how much this means to me."*

Hearing that, I felt a strange mix of relief and happiness. I smiled back at her, wiping my own eyes quickly so she wouldn't see how close I was to breaking down too. *"You mean everything to me, Pari. That's why I wrote it."*

She nodded, her smile growing brighter despite the tears still streaming down her face. *"And you mean everything to me too, Partha. You're my idiot, and I wouldn't trade you for the world."*

That night, we didn't need grand declarations or dramatic gestures. The letter, the tears, and the unspoken understanding between us said it all. It was a moment I'd carry with me forever,a moment that reminded me how deeply we loved each other, and how lucky I was to have her in my life.

That day, when Pari said she wanted to hug me, it was as if my heart skipped a beat. It was the first time she had expressed something so intimate and heartfelt, and it filled me with an indescribable happiness. Her words lingered in my mind, replaying over and over like a melody I didn't want to forget.

I, too, had been longing to hug her ever since the day she confessed her feelings for me. The thought of holding her close, feeling the warmth of her presence, and letting that embrace say everything words couldn't,it was all I wanted. But there was an undeniable barrier between us: the distance.

Physical touch was my love language. A simple hug, a touch on the shoulder, or holding hands meant the world to me. It was how I expressed my emotions most genuinely, and it was how I felt most connected. But with us being apart, that expression of love was out of reach, leaving me yearning for a closeness I couldn't have.

I smiled to myself, imagining what it would be like to finally see her in person. I pictured her running into my arms, the way her hair would sway with the motion, and how her laughter would fill the air as I pulled her into the tightest hug imaginable. I wanted to tell her how much I missed her, not with words, but by holding her close and never letting go.

But for now, I had to settle for her words, her voice, and the love we shared across the distance. Even though it wasn't easy, I reminded myself that every day we spent apart was one step closer to the moment we'd finally be together. And when that moment came, I knew it would be worth the wait.

And soon, that long-awaited moment seemed within reach, as the lockdown restrictions were easing and COVID-19 cases were steadily declining. The world was beginning to open up again, and with it, the possibility of finally seeing Pari in person.

The thought filled me with a mix of excitement and nervousness. For months, we had built our connection through texts, calls, and video chats. We had laughed, cried, and shared our deepest thoughts without ever standing face-to-face. But now, the idea of meeting her felt surreal.

# 2
## When we met...

As the lockdown restrictions eased and travel became possible again, my eagerness to meet Pari grew stronger by the day. Every thought of finally seeing her in person made my heart race with excitement. I had been secretly planning how to bring up the topic of us meeting, carefully crafting the perfect conversation to lay the foundation.

One night, while we were chatting, I decided it was time. I casually brought up the recent news about the lockdown easing. "So, travel restrictions are lifting now, right?" I typed, trying to sound as nonchalant as possible. "Even public transport has started running again."

Pari replied almost instantly, "Yes! Finally, the lockdown is lifting."

I smiled to myself, ready to steer the conversation toward the idea of us meeting. But before I could even type my next message, another text from Pari popped up.

"Finally, we can meet, right? ?"

I froze for a second, staring at her message. My carefully planned conversation crumbled in an instant. She had beaten me to it, voicing exactly what I had been too nervous to say.

I felt a rush of emotions—excitement, relief, and a little bit of embarrassment for overthinking the whole thing. My fingers hovered over the keyboard as I tried to compose myself.

"Exactly what I was about to say!" I replied, adding a smiling emoji to match her energy.

"Really?" Pari replied, followed by a laughing emoji. "I've been waiting for you to bring it up! I thought maybe you didn't want to meet me."

"Are you kidding?" I typed back quickly. "I've been thinking about it for weeks! I just didn't know how to bring it up without sounding too eager."

"Well, now you know," she replied, her text brimming with excitement. "I've been waiting to meet you too. Let's plan it soon!"

That moment felt surreal. The idea of finally meeting her, after all the months of calls, texts, and video chats, was no longer just a dream—it was becoming a reality. And the fact that she was just as excited as I was made it even more special.

As we started discussing the details, I couldn't help but feel a mix of nervousness and joy. This was it—the beginning of a new chapter in our story, one that I knew would bring us even closer.

Now that the idea of meeting was out in the open, we began planning how it would happen. The first big question was: who would travel to whose town? Pari and I went back and forth, considering every possibility.

"Should I come to your town?" I asked tentatively. "It would be easier for you, and I don't mind traveling."

Pari hesitated for a moment. "But if you come here, where will you stay? And how will you explain it to your parents?"

She had a point. The thought of explaining my sudden trip to my parents without revealing the truth about our relationship was daunting. Pari had the same challenge on her side. Our parents didn't know about us yet, and we weren't ready to tell them—not just yet.

"What if you come here?" I suggested. "It might be easier for you since you can say you're visiting old friends or relatives."

Pari thought for a moment. "That's not a bad idea. I do have some old neighbours and relatives in your town. It wouldn't seem suspicious if I said I was visiting them."

"Perfect!" I said, feeling a surge of relief.

But then came the next challenge: where would we meet, and how? We spent the next hour discussing everything from public parks to cafes, trying to figure out the best place to meet for the first time.

"I don't want it to be too crowded," I said. "But it should still be somewhere comfortable where we can talk."

Pari agreed. "And it should be casual. Nothing too fancy or awkward."

Finally, after much debate, we decided on a quiet café near my home. It was cozy, intimate, and just the right setting for our first meeting.

As we finalized the plan, Pari suddenly said, "You know what? I'll come to your town. I've been meaning to visit anyway, and this gives me the perfect excuse. Plus, I really want to see some of my old neighbours and relatives."

Her decision filled me with excitement. The thought of Pari being in my town, just a short distance away, made everything feel real.

"Are you sure?" I asked, trying to hide my growing smile.

"Yes," she said firmly. "I'll let you know once I finalize the dates. But I'm coming, and we're meeting!"

That night, as we said goodnight, I couldn't help but feel a mix of nervous anticipation and overwhelming happiness. The countdown to our first meeting had officially begun.

The anticipation of meeting Pari was almost unbearable. There were still 15 days to go, but each day felt like an eternity. Every time I thought about finally seeing her in person, my heart raced with excitement. Yet, I tried to keep my feelings in check, not wanting to overwhelm her or make things awkward.

Every night, as we chatted, I would imagine what it would be like to see her walk into that café. How her smile would light up the room, how her voice would sound in person, and how it would feel to finally be close to her. But I kept these thoughts to myself, responding to her texts with my usual calm demeanour.

Pari, on the other hand, seemed just as excited but was also trying to play it cool. She would casually mention her travel plans or ask if there were any good places to visit in my town, but I could sense the underlying excitement in her tone.

To distract myself, I started planning everything meticulously. I wanted our first meeting to be perfect. I scouted the café we had chosen, checking out the seating arrangements and imagining where we'd sit. I thought about what I'd wear and even rehearsed a few things I wanted to say to her.

But no matter how much I planned; the waiting was the hardest part. Each day felt slower than the last, and the closer the date got, the more nervous and excited I became.

I didn't want to let Pari know just how eager I was. I didn't want her to feel pressured or to think I was making too big a deal out of it. So, I kept my excitement bottled up, responding to her updates with a casual "That sounds great" or "Can't wait to see you."

But deep down, I was counting down the days, hours, and minutes until I could finally meet the girl who had become my everything.

Three days. Just three days left until I could finally meet Pari. As I was lost in my thoughts, my phone buzzed with a text from her.

"Only three days left, right?" she wrote.

I smiled and replied, "Yes."

What came next took me by surprise.

"Look, I'm done playing it cool. I'm too excited!" Pari texted, followed by a flurry of emojis. "I was holding back because you didn't seem that excited, but I can't anymore. Are you not excited to meet me? I've been dying to see you!"

I couldn't help but laugh softly as I read her message. It was so Pari—straightforward, expressive, and utterly endearing. Her honesty made my heart swell, and I realized how much I loved this about her.

I typed back, "I'm sorry, Maa. I've been just as excited as you, maybe even more. I didn't want to overwhelm you, so I tried to keep it cool too."

Then, deciding it was time to let her know just how much I had been looking forward to this, I added, "I've already been to the café, you know. I checked everything—where we could sit, how the place feels. I've been planning it all."

There was a pause before her next text came in.

"Wait, what? You've already been to the café?!" she replied, followed by a string of laughing emojis. "You're such an idiot, but a cute one. I can't believe you were holding back all this time."

I laughed and wrote back, "I didn't want to make it awkward. But now that you've said it, I can't wait either. These three days feel like forever."

"Same here," she replied. "I've already picked out what I'm going to wear. And you better not mess up when you see me, okay?"

"I won't, Maa. I promise," I wrote back, grinning at the screen.

That conversation made the anticipation even sweeter. Knowing she was just as excited as I was made the wait bearable. And now, those three days couldn't pass quickly enough.

The night before our long-awaited meeting felt like a mix of exhilaration and nervous energy. Every passing second seemed to stretch into an eternity. I was lying on my bed, staring at the ceiling, my phone clutched tightly in my hand as I texted Pari.

"I can't sleep," she texted, followed by a sad emoji.

I chuckled. "You have to sleep, Maa. You need energy for tomorrow. You'll be traveling, and I don't want you to look tired when we meet," I replied, adding a wink emoji.

"But I'm too excited! I keep thinking about tomorrow. What if I forget something important? What if I mess up when I see you?" she wrote back.

"You're not going to mess up," I reassured her. "And even if you do, it's just me, Maa. You can't mess up with me."

She sent a playful eye-roll emoji. "You say that now, but what if I trip or spill something? I'll be so embarrassed!"

I smiled at her text. "I'd find it cute. Besides, I'm more worried about me. What if I see you and forget how to speak? Or worse, say something stupid?"

"Don't worry. You do that every day," she replied with a laughing emoji.

I rolled my eyes at her cheeky reply but felt my heart swell with affection. Even through her texts, I could feel her nervous excitement mirroring my own.

"Okay, but seriously, Maa. Try to sleep. It's almost midnight, and you have to catch the bus early. I don't want you dozing off halfway here," I urged.

"I know, I know. But what about you? Are you sleeping?" she asked.

"I will, once I know you're asleep," I replied.

"That's not fair!" she protested. "You'll stay up all night just to make sure I sleep, won't you?"

"Maybe," I teased.

She sent a string of exasperated emojis but followed it with, "Fine. I'll try to sleep. But you better not look tired tomorrow either!"

"Deal. Now close your eyes and think of Oreo or something," I joked.

"Good night, idiot," she wrote.

"Good night, Maa. Sweet dreams," I replied, though I knew neither of us would be getting much sleep.

As I put my phone down, I realized that the anticipation of seeing her in person, after so many weeks of calls, texts, and video chats, was keeping my heart racing. Tomorrow wasn't just another day—it was the day I'd finally get to see Pari. And that thought was enough to keep me smiling through the sleepless night.

The next morning, I woke up earlier than usual, my heart pounding with excitement. Today was the day. I was finally going to meet Pari in person. I got ready in record time, carefully choosing my outfit—casual but presentable.

As I grabbed my phone to check for her updates, my heart sank. The battery icon glared at me: 7% remaining. In all the excitement last night, I had completely forgotten to charge it. Panic set in. I quickly searched for my power bank, tearing through drawers, bags, and every corner of my room.

Fifteen minutes passed, and I still couldn't find it. My frustration grew with every second. Pari would be traveling, and I couldn't risk my phone dying before we met. Then, as I stood there, catching my breath, a realization hit me like a slap to the face: If I had just plugged my phone in to charge while searching for the power bank, it would have gained at least some battery by now.

I facepalmed, muttering, "Idiot," under my breath. Without wasting another second, I plugged my phone into the charger and sat there, staring at the screen as the battery percentage crawled up painfully slowly.

I texted Pari, "Good morning, Maa. My phone's battery is low, but I'm charging it now. Just a heads-up in case I go silent for a bit."

Her reply came almost instantly. "Good morning, idiot. You're always so careless. How do you manage life without me?"

I chuckled. Even in her teasing, I could feel her care. "I don't manage, Maa. That's why I need you," I replied with a winking emoji.

"Charge your phone properly, okay? I don't want you disappearing on me today!" she warned, adding a playful angry emoji.

"I promise, Maa. I'll be there, fully charged, just like my love for you," I replied, earning a laughing emoji from her.

As the phone charged, I paced around, trying to calm my nerves. The excitement of seeing her for the first time in person was overwhelming, and I wanted everything to be perfect. Little did I know, this small mishap was just the start of a day I'd remember forever.

After about 10–15 minutes, my phone buzzed with a text from Pari: "I'm 10 kilometres away."

My heart started racing. The moment I had been waiting for was almost here. I quickly glanced at my phone battery—53%. It was better than earlier, but I didn't want to risk it running out before or during our meeting. That's when I remembered my mom's power bank.

I walked into the kitchen, where she was busy chopping vegetables for lunch. I tried to act casual, but my excitement was hard to contain.

"Mom, can I borrow your power bank?" I asked, trying to sound nonchalant.

She stopped chopping and looked at me with a curious smile. "Where are you going all dressed up?" she asked, raising an eyebrow.

I froze for a second, quickly crafting a response. "Uh, I'm going to a café with my friends," I said, trying to sound casual but feeling the heat of her gaze.

Her smile widened. "Ohh, okay. But you're looking like a hero today, so I had to ask," she teased, her tone playful.

"Ahhh, stop it, Mom," I replied, my face turning red with embarrassment.

She laughed and handed me the power bank. "Here, hero. Don't forget to return it."

"Thanks, Mom," I said, quickly grabbing it and heading back to my room.

As I plugged the power bank into my phone, I couldn't help but smile. My mom's teasing had eased some of the nervous energy bubbling inside me. But as the minutes ticked by, the excitement of meeting Pari only grew stronger.

I was about to grab the car keys when it hit me—if I took the car, my mom would definitely suspect something was up. She'd already asked me where I was going, and I didn't want to give her any more reasons to question me.

So, I decided to take the scooter instead. It felt like the perfect choice, anyway. The day wasn't too sunny, and there was a pleasant breeze outside. Plus, there's something undeniably romantic about traveling with your loved one on a two-wheeler.

I imagined how it would feel, with Pari sitting behind me, her laughter mixing with the hum of the scooter. The thought made my heart race even more. I grabbed the keys, double-checked my phone and wallet, and headed out, trying to calm my nerves.

As I kickstarted the scooter, I couldn't help but smile. This wasn't just any ride; it was the ride to meet her, the one who had turned my world upside down in the best way possible.

I reached the bus stand and parked the scooter, my heart pounding with anticipation. As I stood there, glancing around nervously, I realized how surreal this moment felt. After only a couple of minutes, the bus arrived—a perfect alignment of timing, as if the universe itself was rooting for us. I didn't have to wait long, but even those two minutes felt like an eternity.

As the bus came to a halt, my emotions surged like a tidal wave. I had met Pari before, but this time was different—this time, she wasn't just my childhood friend; she was my girlfriend. That single word carried so much weight, so much meaning, that I couldn't help but feel overwhelmed.

Excitement coursed through my veins, making my palms sweat. There was a hint of fear too—fear of whether this meeting would be as magical as I'd imagined it. I felt happiness bubbling inside me, a pure and uncontainable joy. And then there was love, a feeling so deep and profound it made everything else fade into the background.

It wasn't just one emotion; it was all of them—excitement, fear, joy, love, and countless others I couldn't even name—all crashing into me at once. My mind raced, my heart thudded, and for a brief moment, I forgot how to breathe.

The doors of the bus opened, and passengers began to step out. My eyes scanned each face, my heart beating faster with every second.

And then I saw her, stepping down from the bus. Pari was wearing a deep, oil-red top paired with black jeans, and a small, fancy backpack slung over her shoulders. The moment I laid eyes on her, my heart skipped a beat, and I froze in place. My body refused to respond, as if every nerve had short-circuited from the sheer intensity of the moment.

She spotted me almost instantly, her face lighting up with a radiant smile that could have stopped time itself. She started walking toward me, and with each step, it felt as though the world around us dissolved into nothingness.

My brain, overwhelmed by the flood of emotions, began processing everything in slow motion. The breeze tousled her hair in the most mesmerizing way, strands dancing around her face like a scene straight out of a movie. Her smile grew wider as she got closer, and I couldn't help but feel as if I were in a dream.

Every detail stood out—the soft glint of sunlight reflecting off her earrings, the rhythmic sound of her footsteps on the pavement, the way her eyes sparkled with excitement. My heart raced, yet time seemed to crawl, stretching each second into an eternity.

In that moment, she wasn't just Pari—she was the girl I'd dreamed of, the one I'd waited for, and now, she was walking toward me, closing the distance that had felt so vast for so long. And as she came closer, her presence broke the spell that had rooted me to the spot.

I was utterly stunned. She was far more beautiful than any of her photos had ever captured. Her presence was almost overwhelming, like a living portrait painted with the most vibrant and delicate strokes. The radiance and glow on her face were indescribable—something words could never do justice to.

What caught my attention next was the small black bindi resting perfectly between her eyebrows. It added an inexplicable charm to her already mesmerizing appearance. It wasn't just an accessory; it felt like it belonged there, accentuating her features and making her look even more ethereal.

As I stood there, frozen in awe, I realized how hopelessly captivated I was. The way she carried herself, the gentle sway of her steps, the effortless grace in her demeanour—it all felt surreal. She wasn't just Pari anymore; she was a vision, a dream brought to life.

I wanted to say something, anything, but my voice seemed to have abandoned me. All I could do was stare, my mind a whirlwind of admiration and disbelief. She smiled again, and that single expression sent waves of warmth through me, making my heart race even faster.

In that moment, I knew—this was her, my Pari, the one who had become the centre of my world. And seeing her like this, in person, was nothing short of magic.

They say love is blind, but in that moment, my eyes had never been wider open. Seeing the love of my life standing before me, every detail of her etched into my memory like a masterpiece, I felt as though the world had stopped spinning just to let me take her in.

Her beauty wasn't just in her appearance; it was in the way she carried herself, the way her eyes sparkled with life, and the way her smile could melt away every worry I'd ever had. She wasn't just someone I loved—she was my entire universe wrapped in one radiant soul.

In that moment, love wasn't blind. It was vivid, overwhelming, and crystal clear. It was the way my heart raced, the way my breath caught, and the way my soul recognized hers as its other half. If this was what love looked like, I never wanted to close my eyes again.

"What are you looking at, idiot?" Pari asked, breaking the silence and snapping me out of the dreamland I had drifted into. Her voice was playful, but it carried the warmth that only she could bring.

I blinked, still trying to process the moment. "I was looking at you, Maa. You're looking gorgeous," I replied, my voice barely above a whisper.

"I know," Pari said with a laugh, her confidence radiating as she teased me.

I could only smile, too stunned to respond further. That was all I could do—stand there, grinning like a fool, utterly flabbergasted by her presence in front of me. The way she looked, the way she laughed, the way she made everything else fade into the background—it was all too much, in the best possible way.

Pari tilted her head slightly, studying me. "You're acting weird," she said, smirking.

"Can you blame me?" I replied, finding just enough composure to tease back. "You've left me speechless."

She laughed again, a sound that felt like music to my ears, and with that, the moment felt perfect. Just us, standing there, the rest of the world forgotten.

"Okay, let's go, come on!" Pari said with her usual enthusiasm, motioning for me to follow her.

Just as I took a step forward, it hit me—I had forgotten something important. My heart skipped a beat as I realized what it was.

"Uh, Pari," I said hesitantly, stopping in my tracks.

She turned to me, raising an eyebrow. "What happened?"

"If you don't mind, can you wait here for a minute? I'll be back in no time," I said, trying to sound casual but knowing I probably looked flustered.

"But why?" she asked, tilting her head slightly, her curiosity piqued.

"Just a minute, Maa," I replied, avoiding her gaze.

She sighed, a mix of confusion and slight amusement on her face. "Okay, fine. But don't take too long."

"Thank you! I'm so sorry—I promise, just one minute!" I said quickly, turning and rushing off before she could ask more questions.

As I hurried away, I could feel her eyes on me, probably wondering what on earth I was up to. But I couldn't let this moment go without fixing my oversight.

I sprinted to the nearby flower shop, my heart pounding—not from the running, but from the realization that I'd forgotten one of the simplest yet most meaningful gestures I'd planned. A rose. I had it all figured out yesterday: as soon as Pari arrived, I'd greet her with a rose and welcome her to the town. But in all the excitement and nerves, I had completely forgotten.

The florist smiled knowingly as I hurriedly grabbed a single, perfect rose. "Special someone?" he asked, handing me the flower.

I nodded, breathless. "Very special," I replied, quickly paying and dashing back toward the bus stand.

As I approached, I slowed down, catching sight of Pari. She was standing there, her hand on her head, shaking it slightly as she watched me with a bemused expression. Her eyes had locked onto the rose in my hand, and I could tell she was trying not to laugh.

"You forgot, didn't you?" she asked as I got closer, her voice carrying a mix of teasing and affection.

I stopped a few steps away from her, catching my breath. "Maybe," I said sheepishly, holding out the rose toward her. "But I remembered now, and that's what counts, right?"

She took the rose, her smile softening as she looked at it. "You're such an idiot," she said, but her tone was filled with warmth.

"Your idiot," I replied with a grin, and for a moment, everything around us seemed to fade away. It was just her, the rose, and the unspoken promise of the day ahead.

"You are such a filmy romantic person, aren't you?" Pari asked, her eyes sparkling with amusement as she twirled the rose between her fingers.

I couldn't help but smile at her teasing tone. "No, no," I said, shaking my head with mock seriousness. "They just use my techniques in their films. I don't copy them."

Pari raised an eyebrow, clearly intrigued by where this was going.

"In fact," I continued, crossing my arms and feigning indignation, "I'm planning to hire some lawyers and file cases against those directors for stealing my ideas. Every romantic gesture they show? Stolen from me."

Pari burst out laughing, her laughter echoing in the air like music. "Oh really? And do you have proof of this grand theft of your so-called techniques?"

I shrugged, pretending to be deep in thought. "Well, the proof is in how impressed you are right now. That's all the evidence I need."

Pari shook her head, still laughing. "You're impossible, you know that?"

"And yet, here you are," I replied with a wink. "Standing next to this impossible guy with a rose in your hand."

She rolled her eyes but smiled even wider. "You're lucky I like impossible people."

"And I'm lucky you're here to laugh at all my ridiculousness," I said softly, feeling the moment settle between us, warm and perfect.

As we walked toward the scooter, I glanced at Pari and said, "By the way, I'm sorry I didn't bring the car. I got my scooty instead. My mom was already looking at me suspiciously while I was getting ready, so..."

Pari stopped and turned to face me, her expression a mix of disbelief and amusement. "Why are you apologizing? Don't tell me you were about to bring the car."

I looked at her, confused. "Uh, yeah? I thought it would be more comfortable for you."

She sighed dramatically, shaking her head. "You forgot, didn't you?"

"Forgot what?" I asked, still clueless.

"I told you when we planned this—bring your scooty. I want to feel the town, the breeze, the vibes. You don't get that in a car!"

Suddenly, it hit me. She *had* said that. I just... completely forgot. I scratched the back of my head sheepishly, feeling a little embarrassed. "Oh... yeah, you did say that."

Pari narrowed her eyes at me, clearly enjoying this moment. "Your brain power is *so* amazing, Partha," she teased, her voice dripping with sarcasm.

I couldn't help but laugh. "What can I say? My mind was preoccupied with... you know, planning the *perfect* welcome."

She smirked, twirling the rose in her hand. "Smooth save, but I'll let it slide. Now, come on, Mr. Forgetful. Let's go explore this town of yours."

As I got on the scooty and turned to Pari, I said, "Hop on."

She smiled, her eyes lighting up with excitement, and then, without hesitation, she placed her hand on my shoulder. The moment her fingers brushed against my skin, I felt a jolt of electricity shoot through me. It was the first time she had touched me, and it felt like the world paused for just a second. My stomach fluttered, and for a brief moment, it felt like my soul had left my body.

She climbed onto the scooty, her touch lingering just a little longer than necessary, and I couldn't help but feel a sense of warmth spread through me.

"Let's go," she said, her voice light and carefree, unaware of the effect she had on me.

I nodded, trying to steady myself, but my heart was racing. "Yeah, let's go," I replied, trying to keep my voice steady, though inside, everything felt like a whirlwind.

With that, I revved up the engine, and as the scooty hummed to life, we started moving. The wind hit our faces, and for a moment, it felt like time had slowed down. With her behind me, her hands lightly resting on my shoulders, I couldn't help but think that this was the beginning of something incredible.

As I navigated through the traffic, I couldn't help but notice how Pari was soaking in the entire vibe of the town. Her eyes sparkled with excitement as she looked around, taking in all the new shops that had popped up since she left. The town, which once felt so familiar, now seemed to have a fresh coat of paint, and I could see the awe in her eyes as she took it all in.

"Look at that!" she exclaimed, pointing to a newly opened café on the corner. "That wasn't here before, was it?" Her voice was filled with wonder as she scanned the street, her eyes flitting from one new building to the next.

"Nope, that's new," I replied, smiling at how excited she was.

She kept on pointing, her hands lightly gripping my shoulders as she looked around, "And that old bookstore, it's gone! I used to love going there." She sighed dramatically, a playful frown on her face. "It's crazy how much things change."

I smiled, enjoying how she was reminiscing about the old days while marvelling at the changes. It was like she was seeing the town with fresh eyes, and I couldn't help but feel proud of the place I called home.

"Yeah, things change," I said, glancing at her with a teasing smile. "But some things, like you, haven't changed a bit."

She raised an eyebrow, looking at me in mock disbelief. "Oh, really?" she said, a smirk tugging at the corner of her lips. "You think I haven't changed?"

I laughed, enjoying the playful banter. "No, not at all. You're still the same—just as beautiful and full of life as ever."

Her cheeks flushed slightly, and she looked away, trying to hide the smile that crept onto her face. "Stop it," she muttered, but I could tell she was secretly pleased.

We continued driving through the town, and with every corner we turned, she pointed out something new, something she remembered, and I couldn't help but feel like this moment—this little adventure through the town—was one I would remember forever.

As we approached the café, a wave of sadness washed over me. I didn't want the ride to end; it had been so perfect, so effortless. The streets, the little banter, the way Pari was enjoying the town—it all felt like something out of a dream. I could almost hear the soundtrack of a movie playing in the background, setting the perfect scene for us.

But as the café came into view, I felt a strange shift in my chest. The excitement of the ride was giving way to a nervousness I couldn't shake. Why was I still afraid? We had been getting along so well, the vibe between us was perfect, yet here I was, feeling the weight of expectation creeping in.

I told myself that sitting here would also be good. I couldn't let my nerves ruin this moment. I had to stop overthinking, stop worrying about messing up. But even with all the pep talk in my head, a small part of me was still anxious.

"Here we are," I said, trying to sound casual as I pulled up to the café. My heart was racing, but I didn't want Pari to see it.

Pari, noticing my slight hesitation, looked at me with a smile. "You okay?" she asked, her voice soft but laced with concern.

I nodded quickly, trying to hide the nervousness in my eyes. "Yeah, just... a little overwhelmed. It's just been a really great day, you know?"

She smiled warmly, understanding what I meant. "I get it," she said, her tone reassuring. "But hey, we're here now. No pressure, just us, a coffee, and some good conversation."

Her words made me feel a little lighter. Maybe I was making this into a bigger deal than it needed to be. I took a deep breath, reminding myself that this was exactly what I wanted—this time with her, this moment.

"Right," I said, giving her a small smile. "Let's go."

We got off the scooty, and as we walked towards the café, I couldn't help but feel a mix of excitement and nervousness. I opened the door for her, and she looked at me with that smile—warm, genuine, and full of understanding. My heart skipped a beat as she stepped inside, and I followed her in, trying to keep my composure.

I quickly scanned the café for a spot, and by some stroke of luck, the table I had my eye on was empty. Without wasting a second, I hurried over and pulled out the chair for her. "Please, sit," I gestured, feeling a bit like a nervous host at my own little event.

Pari paused for a moment, looking at me with an amused expression. "You're way too filmy, Partha," she said, her voice filled with playful teasing.

I chuckled, feeling a little embarrassed but also proud of my effort. "Hey, what can I say? I'm just trying to impress you," I replied with a wink, trying to brush off the awkwardness.

She laughed softly, shaking her head. "Impressing me, huh? You're doing a good job so far."

I grinned and gestured for her to sit down again. "Well, that's a relief. I was worried my filmy moves wouldn't work on you."

She smiled and sat down, her eyes sparkling with amusement. As we settled into our seats, I felt a little more at ease. The tension from earlier was melting away, replaced by the comfort of just being with her. The café felt cozy, and everything about the moment seemed to align perfectly.

"Okay, now that I've got you here," I said, leaning in slightly, "what are you having? I'm thinking something sweet, because today's been pretty sweet so far."

Pari raised an eyebrow, her playful smile never leaving her face. "You're really setting the bar high, huh?"

I shrugged with a grin. "I like to aim high."

We both laughed, and for the first time that day, I felt completely at ease, the nerves that had plagued me earlier fading into the background. It was just me and Pari, in this little café, enjoying each other's company. And in that moment, everything felt just right.

I ordered a cappuccino and a coffee-flavoured brownie, savouring the thought of the rich, comforting Flavors. Pari, on the other hand, went for a KitKat milkshake and a couple of cupcakes, her choices reflecting her sweet and playful nature. Once we'd placed our orders, she looked at me with a curious expression.

"What's the deal with that thing between you and coffee?" she asked, her voice teasing. "You ordered coffee and a coffee-flavoured brownie. Do you have some secret love affair with coffee or something?"

I grinned, leaning back in my chair. "I love coffee," I replied, keeping my tone casual. "More than you," she teased, raising an eyebrow.

I chuckled, shaking my head. "No, no. If I had to choose between you and a cappuccino, I would definitely choose you, Maa," I said, my voice softening a little as I spoke the words.

Her eyes twinkled with amusement, and she leaned back in her seat, pretending to consider my answer. "Oh, well, that's okay then," she said, her smile widening.

I couldn't resist. "But," I added with a mischievous grin, "if I had to choose between you and an authentic filter coffee, I think I'd take the coffee."

Pari's eyes widened in mock shock, and she gasped dramatically. "Excuse me?" she asked, her voice playful but with a hint of mock indignation. "Are you saying coffee beats me?"

I laughed, raising my hands in mock surrender. "Okay, okay, I'm just joking! You're definitely more important than any cup of coffee. But, you know, filter coffee does have a special place in my heart."

She rolled her eyes, but the smile never left her face. "You're impossible," she said, shaking her head, but I could tell she was enjoying the playful banter.

"I know," I replied, leaning in slightly. "But I think that's part of my charm."

Pari laughed, and for a moment, everything felt easy. The tension from earlier was gone, replaced by the warmth of the moment, the shared jokes, and the comfort of each other's company. As we waited for our drinks and treats, I couldn't help but think that this was exactly how I imagined our first meeting—playful, easy, and filled with laughter.

We spent around two hours at the cafe, talking, laughing, and losing track of time. It felt like the world had slowed down, and it was just the two of us, wrapped in our own little bubble of happiness. As the conversation flowed, I couldn't help but feel how natural it all was, like we had been talking for years instead of just meeting in person for the first time.

But eventually, Pari checked her watch and reminded me that she still had to meet some of her relatives and old neighbours. That was the reason she had told her parents about the visit in the first place. I could see the slight shift in her energy as she prepared to leave, and I didn't want to hold her back from those visits, so I offered to drop her off.

She had to visit about 7 or 8 houses that day, and as much as I wanted to stay by her side, I knew it was important for her to reconnect with the people she hadn't seen in a while. "Come with me," she suggested as we stood up from the table.

I smiled, shaking my head. "No, you go ahead. I'll wait outside. You should catch up with everyone. I'll be here when you're done."

She looked at me for a moment, her expression softening, and then nodded. "Alright, but don't go anywhere," she teased, giving me a playful wink.

I laughed and promised I wouldn't. As she walked off to the first house, I stood there for a moment, watching her disappear into the distance. There was something so peaceful about just waiting for her, knowing that soon, I'd see her again. It was a strange feeling—waiting for someone you care about, but it felt right. It felt like I was exactly where I was meant to be.

As the hours passed, I found myself lost in my thoughts, occasionally checking my phone, but mostly just enjoying the calm of the day. I couldn't wait to hear all about her visits, the stories she'd share, and the memories she'd reconnect with. But for now, I was content to wait. After all, we had all the time in the world.

By the time the evening had arrived, I found myself sitting outside my father's restaurant, my thoughts completely consumed by Pari. The day had gone by faster than I expected, and I couldn't help but replay every moment from when we first met until now. There was something so special about being with her, something that made me forget about everything else in the world.

I had already planned the evening near the riverbank, a peaceful spot I knew would be perfect for us to unwind after her busy day of visiting relatives. I had told her to come back before sunset, so we could enjoy the view together. The idea of sitting by the river, talking, and just being in each other's company seemed like the perfect way to end our first day together.

At 5:30, my phone rang, pulling me out of my thoughts. It was Pari.

"I'm finished visiting. Come and pick me up," she said, her voice light but full of excitement.

I smiled, feeling a rush of anticipation. "I'll be there in a minute," I replied, already standing up and heading toward the door of the restaurant.

As I made my way to the car, I couldn't help but feel that familiar flutter in my chest. The thought of spending more time with Pari, especially at the riverbank, made me feel like I was walking on air. I knew the evening would be perfect—just the two of us, surrounded by the calmness of the river and the fading light of the setting sun.

As soon as I arrived and saw Pari standing there, I honked the horn lightly. She looked up and immediately spotted me, walking towards the car with a smile that made my heart skip a beat.

"Where's your scooty? Why did you bring your car?" she asked, her curiosity piqued.

I smiled, trying to sound casual. "I'll get cold, Maa. You'll feel sick if you ride on the scooty in the evening. And to watch the sunset in the car is peaceful—you can sit comfortably in the seats, no bumps or wind in your face."

Pari raised an eyebrow, but then she nodded, clearly appreciating the comfort of the car. "Hmm, I see," she said, sliding into the passenger seat with a grin. "You're always thinking ahead, aren't you?"

I chuckled as I started the engine, feeling a rush of excitement. The evening was unfolding just as I had hoped—calm, peaceful, and full of moments that I knew would stay with me forever. As I drove toward the riverbank, I couldn't help but steal glances at Pari, the girl who had somehow become the centre of my world in such a short time.

As I drove, I smiled at her excitement. "Okay, it's fine to watch the sunset from the car, but I have to go near the river and play," Pari said, her voice filled with determination.

I couldn't help but laugh. "Alright, I'll take you to the river, but not for long—you'll get sick," I warned, though I knew it was probably a lost cause.

We arrived at the riverbank, and as soon as I parked the car, Pari jumped out with a burst of energy. She ran toward the water, kicking off her shoes, and without a second thought, she splashed some water in my direction, her laughter ringing through the air.

"Pari! Stop, Maa, please, it's cold!" I said, wiping the water off my face, but she just giggled, clearly enjoying herself.

She splashed again, her eyes sparkling with mischief. "Come on, Partha! It's fun!" she teased, completely carefree, her playful energy contagious.

I couldn't help but smile, even as I pretended to be annoyed. "You're going to make me sick with all this water, Pari!" I said, but deep down, I loved seeing her so happy, so full of life.

Her laughter was like music to my ears, and for a moment, everything else faded away. It was just the two of us, the river, and the sound of her playful joy filling the air.

We walked back to the car, both of us still laughing from the playful moments by the river. As we reached the bonnet, I sat down and patted the space next to me, signalling for Pari to join. She climbed up beside me, and we both leaned back, watching the sunset slowly paint the sky in shades of pink and orange.

"It's so peaceful, right?" I said, my voice soft, taking in the beauty of the moment.

"Yeah, and also so beautiful," Pari replied, her eyes fixed on the horizon, a content smile on her face.

"Yeah, just like you," I said, unable to resist the urge to compliment her.

Pari turned to me with a playful glare. "Stop it, idiot. You've already impressed me. Why are you doing it again?"

I chuckled, my heart swelling with affection. "I'll always be like this around you, Maa. You're the best thing that happened to my life," I said, my voice sincere, a hint of a smile tugging at my lips.

She looked at me, her expression softening, and for a moment, there was a silence between us, filled with nothing but the sounds of the evening breeze and the fading sunlight. It felt like time had stopped, and it was just the two of us, lost in our little world.

As the last rays of the sun disappeared, leaving behind a blanket of darkness, the peaceful silence between us lingered. We sat there for a while, the world around us quiet, as if it was waiting for us to make the next move. I could feel the weight of the moment, knowing that the day was coming to an end.

Reluctantly, I stood up from the bonnet and offered my hand to Pari. She took it, and we walked back to the car, both of us a little quieter than before, the reality of the evening's end settling in.

The drive to the bus stand felt different now, like every mile was stretching longer, and the air between us felt heavier. I could feel the bittersweetness in the silence. This was the part I had been dreading—saying goodbye.

"Pari," I said, breaking the silence, my voice low, "I really enjoyed today. It was perfect."

She smiled softly, but I could see the sadness in her eyes. "Yeah, me too. It was... amazing. I didn't want it to end."

"I know," I replied, my heart heavy. "But we'll see each other again soon, right?"

"Of course," she said, her voice filled with warmth, but there was a slight hesitation. "We'll make more memories."

I nodded, trying to push back the lump in my throat. The bus stand was in sight now, and I could see the bus waiting, ready to take her back. We pulled up, and I parked the car. The moment had come.

"I'll miss you, Pari," I said quietly, looking at her.

"I'll miss you too, Partha," she replied, her voice trembling slightly. She reached for the door handle but paused for a moment, turning back to look at me.

Before she got out, I leaned over and gave her a quick, gentle hug, holding on just a little longer than I meant to. "Take care of yourself, okay?" I whispered.

"I will. You too," she whispered back.

With a final smile, she stepped out of the car, her hand brushing mine as she closed the door. I watched her walk towards the bus, my heart feeling heavy but full of love. As she turned one last time, I waved, and she waved back, her smile lighting up the darkness around us.

And just like that, she was gone. But the memories of today, of us, would stay with me forever.

As the bus slowly pulled away, its headlights cutting through the evening darkness, I found myself rooted to the spot, watching it disappear into the distance. My heart felt heavy, a strange mix of longing and satisfaction swirling inside me. I had spent the most magical day with Pari, yet the reality of her leaving was harder than I had anticipated.

The thought of following the bus crossed my mind—a fleeting impulse to stay close to her for just a little longer.

But I stopped myself, knowing it would only make the goodbye more difficult for her. She needed to leave with the memories of a perfect day, not with me chasing after her like someone unwilling to let go.

Instead, I stood there, hands in my pockets, watching the taillights fade into the horizon. I took a deep breath, the cool evening air filling my lungs, and smiled softly to myself. Pari had brought so much light into my life, and today was a testament to that.

As I turned back to my car, I whispered under my breath, "See you soon, Maa." Then, with one last glance at the road, I got into the car and drove away, carrying the warmth of her presence in my heart, knowing this was just the beginning of our journey together.

As I drove back, my phone buzzed with a notification. I pulled over to check it, and there it was—a message from Pari.

*"Thank you for everything today. You made this day so memorable; I won't forget it in my life. By spending this one day with you, I can't even imagine how happy I'll be when I get to spend every day with you. I love you so much, Partha."*

Reading her words, my chest tightened, and my eyes welled up. Her message carried so much love, sincerity, and hope that I couldn't help but feel overwhelmed. It was as if all the emotions I had kept in check throughout the day had finally found their way to the surface.

But I didn't want her to know I was tearing up. I wanted to keep the moment light for her. So, I quickly typed back:

*"It was great spending time with you too, Maa. Today was truly special."*

I stared at the screen for a moment after sending it, smiling through the tears. Her love felt so pure, so real, and I couldn't wait for the day when we wouldn't have to say

**goodbye anymore.**

# 3

## When Distance Grew...

That meeting brought Pari and me closer than ever. The next morning, as I opened my eyes, my phone buzzed with a notification. Groggily, I reached for it and saw a message from Pari:

*"Still dreaming about me, idiot?"*

I chuckled. It was so typical of her playful, teasing, and full of life.

*"No, I was dreaming about coffee,"* I replied, smirking to myself.

I knew exactly what I was doing. Just the day before, she'd been mock-angry when I joked about loving coffee more than her.

As expected, a furious emoji popped up on my screen almost instantly.

*"You're impossible, Partha!"* she replied, followed by another string of angry emojis.

I couldn't help but laugh. Pari's playful annoyance was one of the things I loved most about her. It was our little game, and it made every day brighter.

*"Okay, okay, Maa. You win. Coffee can't compete with you. Happy now?"* I sent back, trying to appease her.

*"Better,"* she replied, adding a smug emoji.

And just like that, my day had started with Pari's mischief and her infectious energy. It was perfect.

So, I thought of making day even better by calling her and hearing voice. As she picked up the call and said hello. Her voice kind of felt off.

Hearing Pari's voice like that, I immediately knew something was off. She had been texting me like her usual playful self, but now her voice carried a weight of sadness, as if she had just stopped crying.

*"What happened, Maa?"* I asked gently, trying not to sound too alarmed.

*"Nothing,"* Pari replied, her voice barely above a whisper.

But I wasn't convinced. I knew her too well to let it slide.

*"I know something's wrong. Tell me, Maa. Please,"* I urged her.

There was a pause on the other end, and then she finally spoke, her voice trembling.

*"I miss you so much, Partha. Yesterday was so perfect, and today... I just wish we could have another day like that. I want to be with you again, right now."*

Her words hit me like a wave. My heart ached knowing she was feeling this way, and I couldn't be there to hold her or comfort her.

*"Maa,"* I said softly, *"I miss you too. More than you can imagine. Yesterday was one of the best days of my life, and I wish I could make every day like that for you."*

There was silence for a moment, and then I heard her sniffle.

*"You mean that?"* she asked, her voice fragile but hopeful.

*"Of course, Maa. If I could, I'd be there with you right now. But until then, we'll make the most of every moment we have, even if it's over the phone. I'm always here for you, Pari.*

*Always."*

Her breathing steadied, and I could feel her calming down.

*"Thank you, Partha,"* she said softly. *"I don't know what I'd do without you."*

*"You'll never have to find out,"* I replied, my voice firm but full of warmth.

We stayed on the call for a while, talking about everything and nothing, until her laughter returned, and I could finally hear the smile in her voice again.

From that day forward, I realized something important about Pari, she had a way of masking her sadness behind normal texts. If I wasn't careful, I might miss it. Her words might seem fine, but her tone was the real giveaway. It became clear to me that I needed to pay closer attention to the patterns in her texts and, more importantly, call her more often.

I've always preferred calls over texts anyway. Texts are convenient, sure, but they leave too much room for misunderstanding. You can't hear the emotion behind the words, the subtle shifts in tone, or the pauses that convey so much. A simple "I'm fine" over text can mean a hundred different things, but hearing it in her voice makes all the difference.

Calling her frequently became my way of ensuring our relationship stayed healthy. It wasn't just about checking in; it was about truly connecting. I wanted to hear her laugh, her excitement, her dreams, and even her worries. Texts could never capture the way her voice softened when she was being affectionate or the playful edge when she was teasing me.

I made a promise to myself: no matter how busy life got, I would always find time to call her, to hear her voice, and to make sure she felt loved and understood. For me, those calls weren't just conversations; they were lifelines that kept us close, even when distance tried to come between us.

Everything was going so perfectly between us that it felt like we were destined to be together. According to Indian lore, the formation of a pearl is considered a celestial phenomenon blessed by the gods. During the Swathi Nakshatra—a specific constellation in the sky, rain falls into the ocean, and oysters open up to welcome the drops. The right drop finds the right oyster and transforms into a precious pearl.

In many ways, our story felt like that divine alignment. I found Pari, the right person for me, and I knew deep down that I would strive to be the right person for her. Like the pearl and the oyster, we complemented each other, and together, we were creating something beautiful—something rare and cherished.

Pari brought out the best in me, and I hoped I did the same for her. It wasn't just love; it was a connection that felt cosmic, as if the universe had conspired to bring us together under the right stars at the right time. And just like the pearl, our bond grew stronger and more valuable with each moment we spent together.

Now that the lockdown restrictions had eased, my friends and I decided it was finally time to catch up. Despite living in the same city, I had been so consumed by my love story with Pari that I hadn't made time to meet them. Determined to reconnect, I decided to call my childhood friend, Anni, to plan a get-together.

As the phone rang, Anni picked up almost immediately. "Oh, it's Partha the Great! I thought you forgot I existed," he said sarcastically.
"Shut up, Anni," I replied with a laugh. "Tomorrow, I'll be at

your place. Let's meet at our adda."

Our adda was a hotel that had become our unofficial hangout spot over the years. It wasn't fancy or extravagant, but it was ours. The highlight was the small counter outside the hotel, right in the parking lot, where we would sip tea and lose track of time while chatting about everything and nothing.

"Done!" Anni said enthusiastically. "I'll call the others. Be there on time, though. It's not college to come after 10 minutes"

I laughed, knowing he was teasing but also acknowledging the truth in his words. It had been far too long since I'd spent time with my friends, and I was genuinely excited to relive those carefree moments with them.

To make the catch-up even more exciting, I decided to call Jai, one of my high school friends. Along with Anni, he was one beside Anni who knew about my story with Pari. However, they both thought my connection with Pari was casual and had no idea we were actually in a relationship. They didn't even know how much we had been talking, let alone that we had recently met in person.

As I spoke to Jai, he was thrilled about the plan.
"Finally, Partha! You're coming out of hiding. I was starting to think someone had kidnapped you or something," he joked.
"Yeah, yeah, very funny," I replied. "Be there tomorrow at the adda. It's been ages since we all caught up."

What Jai didn't know was that I had a little surprise planned. During my meet-up with Pari at the café, we had taken a photo together, a memory I cherished. I decided to use that photo to break the news to them about our relationship.

I could already imagine their reactions. Anni and Jai had been rooting for me and Pari for a long time, even when they thought it was just a casual connection. Revealing that we were now officially together, and seeing their faces when they realized how serious it had become, was going to be priceless.

I smiled to myself, already looking forward to the next day. It wasn't just going to be a reunion with friends, it was going to be a moment to share my happiness with them.

Next day As I walked up to our tea spot, a little late at 11:10 AM, I could see Anni and Jai already waiting for me. Both of them had their arms crossed, giving me a mock-angry glare.

"Look who decided to show up!" Anni started, his tone dripping with sarcasm.

"Do you even value our time, Partha?" Jai chimed in, pretending to be offended.

They both started scolding me for being late, their exaggerated expressions making me laugh internally. I didn't say a word, though. Instead, I casually pulled out my phone, unlocked it, and opened the photo of me and Pari from the café. Without a word, I held it up for them to see.

Their reactions were exactly as I had imagined.

"Shut up!" Anni exclaimed, his eyes wide with disbelief. "When did this happen, dude?!"

Jai, equally stunned, leaned closer to the phone. "Wait... is this from a few days ago? Like, recently?"

"Yeah," I replied, grinning ear to ear. "Day before yesterday."

For a moment, they were both speechless, just staring at the photo. Then Anni broke the silence.

"Partha, you sly dog! You didn't tell us you were actually meeting her!"

"I wanted to surprise you," I said, chuckling.

Jai shook his head in disbelief. "You're unbelievable. And this photo... you guys look so happy. So, it's official now?"

"Yeah," I said, my smile widening. "We're together."

Anni and Jai erupted into cheers and started teasing me relentlessly, but I could see the genuine happiness in their eyes. It felt amazing to share this moment with them. This wasn't just about revealing my relationship with Pari, it was about celebrating it with two of my closest friends.

After a few minutes of chatting with Anni and Jai, I decided to call a few more friends to join us. They didn't know about Pari yet, and I thought it would be fun to keep that surprise for later. So, I picked up my phone and called Sai, Mithun, Pratham, Siddu, Swasthik, and Roopal, asking them to come over to our tea spot.

Within ten minutes, they all started showing up, one by one, each of them bringing their own energy and excitement. It had been a long time since we all gathered like this, and the atmosphere quickly became lively.

We sat around the counter, sipping tea and chatting for hours. Stories from school days, updates on life, and random jokes filled the air. It was refreshing to reconnect with them, especially after being so absorbed in my relationship with Pari.

By the end of the day, we all agreed that meeting like this should become a routine. We decided to catch up daily for an hour, just to unwind and talk about whatever was on our minds.

For me, it felt perfect. It gave me a balance, a chance to reconnect with my boys and indulge in some carefree "boys' talk," while also cherishing the bond I had with Pari. Life was starting to feel like it was falling perfectly into place.

As I reached home, feeling content after a great day with my friends, I decided to call Pari.

"Hoo, Mr. Partha," Pari said in her usual playful tone as soon as she picked up the call.

"Yepppp," I replied, matching her energy.

"So, how was your day with your friends?" she asked curiously.

"It was fabulous! Anni and Jai were in utter shock when they found out about us," I said with a chuckle, remembering their stunned faces.

"Oh, is it? What about the others?" she asked.

"I didn't tell them yet," I admitted. "I'll probably let them know after a week or so. I wanted to ease into it."

"Ah, keeping secrets now, are we?" Pari teased.

"Not really. I just thought it'd be fun to build up to it. Besides, I wanted to enjoy today without making it all about us," I explained.

"Fair enough," she replied, laughing softly. "But make sure you tell them soon. I don't want to be your little secret forever!"

"Of course, maa. You're not a secret; you're my highlight," I said with a grin, even though she couldn't see it.

We spent the rest of the call talking about our day, sharing little moments and jokes. It felt good to end the day hearing her voice, knowing she was as much a part of my life as my friends were

As the days went by, our group of friends started meeting up regularly. The bond we shared grew even stronger, and it felt like old times again. After about two weeks, I finally told everyone about Pari.

The moment they found out, the teasing began, and it didn't stop. Every time we met, they would find a way to slip her name into the conversation.

"Do you even get time from your *wife* now?" Sai would ask, grinning mischievously.

"Bro, does Pari give you a hall pass to hang out with us, or do we need to get her approval?" Mithun would add, making everyone laugh.

I acted like the teasing was annoying, rolling my eyes and shaking my head. "Oh, come on, guys. Can we talk about something else for once?" I'd say, trying to keep a straight face.

But deep down, their teasing felt good. It wasn't just harmless fun; it was their way of showing they were happy for me. Every joke, every sarcastic comment, made me realize how much they cared. It was their way of accepting Pari as a part of my life, and that meant everything to me.

Even when they called her my "wife," it brought a smile to my face. I might have acted like I was annoyed, but honestly, I loved it. Their teasing turned into a constant reminder of how lucky I was to have Pari in my life.

After all the excitement with Pari and reconnecting with my childhood friends, I realized I had completely neglected my only two female friends from college, Advaya and Sowmika. Feeling a little guilty, I decided to text them both to catch up.

"Hey," I typed, keeping it simple.

Advaya replied almost immediately, "Hello." Short and sweet, just like her usual self.

Sowmika, on the other hand, came in with her typical dramatic flair. "Ho, it's Partha! After all this time, I thought you forgot me, mister! By the way, I am Sowmika," she replied.

I couldn't help but laugh at her reply. That was so like her—always adding a touch of drama to every conversation.

I replied, "Oh, come on, Sowmika. How could I forget you? You're unforgettable, just like your dramatic introductions!"

"And what about me?" Advaya chimed in, clearly not wanting to be left out.

"Advaya, you're my calm in the storm of Sowmika's theatrics," I replied, trying to balance things out.

We chatted for a while, catching up on life and reminiscing about our college days. It felt good to reconnect with them, and I realized how much I had missed their energy and unique personalities.

Life had settled into a rhythm that felt surprisingly good, considering the world outside was still recovering from the lockdown. Some days stretched endlessly, making every hour feel like a test of patience, while others seemed to vanish in the blink of an eye.

But no matter how the days unfolded, talking to Pari was the constant that kept me grounded. Her voice, her texts, and our playful banter made everything brighter, even on the dullest days. Meeting up with my friends regularly added another layer of joy, it felt like I was rediscovering the essence of friendship and the simple pleasures of life.

The lockdown restrictions were still a shadow over everything, but somehow, it didn't matter as much anymore. Pari and my friends had turned what could have been a monotonous phase into a time filled with laughter, connection, and warmth.

It felt like life was moving forward, not just in big leaps but in small, meaningful steps. And in those moments, I realized that even amidst uncertainty, it was possible to find happiness in the little things, the people you love, the conversations you cherish, and the memories you create together.

After some days the news of the board exams being cancelled was a surprise that left most of us thrilled. After months of disrupted schedules and zero focus on studies, this felt like a blessing in disguise. I immediately picked up my phone to share the excitement with Pari.

"Pari, did you hear? The exams are cancelled! No more late-night cramming or last-minute revisions," I exclaimed.

But to my surprise, Pari didn't share my enthusiasm. Her voice on the other end sounded more subdued. "Yeah, I heard," she said, almost reluctantly.

"What's wrong? Why aren't you happy?" I asked, genuinely puzzled.

"I only got 87% in my first PU," she confessed. "And now that's going to decide my board percentage too. I didn't study properly because everyone said the first PU doesn't matter. Now I'm stuck with it."

Her disappointment was evident, and suddenly, I realized my situation wasn't all that different. My first PU performance wasn't stellar either, I had barely managed something in the 70s. This meant my board percentage would reflect that too.

"Pari, I get it," I said, trying to reassure her. "But think about it, this isn't the end. It's just one milestone. We can still prove ourselves in the future, whether it's college or wherever life takes us."

She sighed, and I could sense her trying to come to terms with it. "I guess you're right. It's just... I wanted to do better."

"And you will," I said confidently. "This is just a small bump. Besides, you're way ahead of me. You've got nothing to worry about compared to my disaster of a percentage!"

She let out a small laugh, and I knew I'd managed to lighten her mood a little. Sometimes, all it took was perspective and a bit of humour to navigate the uncertainties. And in that moment, even with the shadow of disappointment, we found a way to look forward together.

A few days after our conversation, another announcement came through that changed everything: the entrance exams would not take board exam percentages into account. This was a huge relief, especially for Pari, who had been upset about her first PU marks.

I immediately called her. "See, Maa? I told you not to stress too much. Now you can focus on the entrance exam and still get into a great college," I said, my voice brimming with optimism.

Pari chuckled on the other end. "You're right, Partha. But honestly, do you think the entrance exams will even happen? It's been eight months of lockdown already. They might just cancel those too."

Her words echoed what I'd been secretly thinking. The pandemic had thrown everything into disarray, and it felt like nothing was certain anymore. The idea of entrance exams being cancelled didn't seem far-fetched.

"Maybe you're right," I said, leaning into her theory. "But just in case, we should at least pretend to study, right? You know, so we don't get caught off guard."

"Pretend to study?" she laughed. "That sounds like your specialty, Partha!"

"Hey, I'm serious!" I replied, trying to sound offended but failing to hide my grin.

In truth, neither of us felt the urgency to prepare. The endless lockdown had dulled our sense of time and urgency, and we were riding on the hope that the exams might not happen at all.

Later that day, Pari called me, her voice bubbling with excitement.

"Partha, you know what? I have a wonderful idea!" she exclaimed.

I had no clue what she was talking about, so I asked, "What idea, Maa?"

"We'll study together and aim to go to the same college! Even if one of us gets a slightly lower rank, we'll still try to get into the same college, even if it's in different branches. We can always apply for a branch change after the first year, right?"

For a moment, I was speechless. Pari's enthusiasm was contagious, but deep down, I knew the reality of my academic abilities. I wasn't as focused or naturally brilliant as she was. The idea of us ending up in the same college felt more like a dream than a plan.

"Pari, that's a great idea," I said cautiously, not wanting to dampen her spirits. "But you know me. Even if I study, I probably won't get the kind of rank you will. You're way ahead of me."

"Stop it, Partha," she interrupted. "Don't sell yourself short. If we study together, we'll motivate each other. You'll do better than you think. And anyway, it's not just about ranks. It's about us being together."

Her words made my heart swell. She had so much faith in me, even when I doubted myself.

"Alright, Maa," I said, smiling. "Let's do it. Same college, same campus. But you'll have to promise me one thing."

"What?" she asked curiously.

"That you won't get annoyed when I ask you to explain everything to me a hundred times."

She laughed. "Deal! But only if you promise not to give up halfway through."

"Promise," I said, feeling a renewed sense of determination.

From that moment, the idea of us being together in college became a shared dream. It wasn't just about studying anymore; it was about building a future together, one step at a time.

The next day, I woke up earlier than usual, which was a rare sight in my house, thanks to the lockdown and my late-night chats with Pari. As I rummaged through my room, looking for my long-forgotten books, my mom walked in and froze, staring at me like she'd just seen a ghost.

"You're up early?" she asked, her voice dripping with suspicion.

"Yeah," I replied nonchalantly, still searching.

"What are you looking for?" she asked again.

"My books," I said, not even glancing at her. "Have you seen them?"

For a moment, there was silence. Then, she burst out laughing. "What is happening today? You woke up early, and now you're looking for books? Did the sun rise in the west?"

I rolled my eyes. "From today, your son will be studying two hours daily. Don't disturb me, okay?" I said with mock seriousness.

"Two hours? Wow! Should I call the newspaper and tell them about this miracle?" she teased.

"Very funny, Ma," I said, finally finding my books under a pile of old notebooks.

She walked away, still laughing, but I could see the amused pride in her eyes. Little did she know that my sudden dedication to studies wasn't entirely self-motivated, it was Pari-motivated.

At 10 a.m., Pari called, right on time. "Ready, Mr. Scholar?" she asked cheerfully.

"As ready as I'll ever be," I replied, opening my dusty books.

And just like that, our study sessions began. It wasn't just about the books or the exams anymore—it was about spending time together, supporting each other, and building the dream we had decided to chase.

After an hour of studying with Pari, my brain felt like it was overheating. I wanted to spend time with her, but the studies were going way over my head. I tried to focus, but the words in the books seemed to blur together, and all I could think about was how much easier life could be.

Finally, I couldn't hold it in anymore. "Pari," I said, breaking the silence.

"Yes, Partha?" she replied, her tone calm and focused.

"I have another brilliant idea," I said, trying to sound enthusiastic.

"What now?" she asked, a hint of suspicion in her voice.

"Listen, you study hard and join the college through the entrance exams. I'll just get a management seat in the same college. That way, I won't even have to worry about changing branches later!" I said, feeling proud of my 'genius' plan.

There was a pause on the other end of the call. Then Pari sighed deeply. "Partha," she said slowly, "you're unbelievable."

"What? It's a good plan!" I defended myself.

"Good plan for you, maybe!" she replied, laughing. "You're just trying to escape studying, aren't you?"

"Not escape," I said, grinning. "I'm just being practical. Why go through all the stress when we have another option?"

She laughed again, her voice filled with warmth. "You're impossible. But fine, do what you want. Just don't expect me to stop teasing you about it later."

"Deal," I said, relieved.

Even though I wasn't the most diligent student, I knew one thing for sure, no matter what, I wanted to be with Pari. And if that meant taking the easier route to get to the same destination, I was all in.

A few days later, the exam dates were announced, and the entire student community collectively groaned. It was as if the universe had conspired against us, pulling us out of our cozy, lockdown-induced laziness.

Despite the announcement, no one, including Pari, seemed to take the exams seriously. Pari, who was usually disciplined, studied for just two hours a day. Even though I tried to encourage her to put in more effort, it was clear that the rhythm of studying had been lost for months. The lockdown had drained everyone's academic motivation.

Whenever I called Pari to check on her progress, our conversations would inevitably drift away from studies. "So, how much did you study today?" I'd ask.

"Two hours," she'd reply, sounding unbothered. "But I spent more time deciding what to eat for lunch than actually studying."

I couldn't blame her. I was no better. My own books were gathering dust again, and I found myself making excuses to avoid opening them. "It's not like we can learn an entire syllabus in a few weeks," I'd tell myself.

Group chats were filled with memes about last-minute studying and the collective struggle of students trying to remember how to hold a pen. Everyone seemed to be in the same boat, floating somewhere between procrastination and panic.

One day, while on a call, Pari said, "You know, Partha, even if we don't score great, it's fine. We'll figure things out. What matters is that we're trying."

Her words comforted me, and I realized that maybe she was right. While the exams loomed over us, the world was still healing from a pandemic. Perhaps it wasn't just about marks anymore, it was about resilience and adapting to the unexpected.

Even with minimal preparation, we knew we'd face the exams together, supporting each other through whatever came next.

Finally, the day of the exams arrived, and I found myself at the exam center, more out of obligation than any real intent to excel. I had barely studied, so my plan was simple: participate for the sake of it.

As I sat in the exam hall and received the question paper, I glanced through it. It was as if the paper was written in some ancient script. I didn't know a single answer. My first thought was to randomly mark answers on the OMR sheet and leave, but then I noticed a rule: we had to remain in the exam hall for the full 2.5 hours.

"Great," I thought sarcastically. "Now what am I supposed to do?"

With nothing better to do, I decided to pass the time by reading the questions. As I started going through them, I found myself unconsciously marking the options that felt right to me. It wasn't based on logic or memory, just pure gut feeling.

For every subject, I repeated the same process. Read the question, skim the options, and let my instincts guide me. It felt oddly liberating. There was no pressure, no expectations, just me and my random guesses.

By the end of the exams, I walked out of the hall feeling surprisingly relaxed. I wasn't sure how well I'd done, but I also didn't care too much. I knew I had done my part, no matter how unconventional it was.

Later that evening, when I called Pari, she asked, "So, how was the exam?"

I laughed and said, "It was like playing a game of 'Who Wants to Be a Millionaire?' Except I didn't have any lifelines."

Pari chuckled. "Well, at least you participated. That's more than some people can say."

In that moment, I realized that, no matter the outcome, the experience itself was worth something. It was a reminder that sometimes, simply showing up and trying, even if imperfectly, is an achievement in itself.

With the exams finally behind me, it felt like a huge weight had been lifted, even though I hadn't taken them seriously in the first place. Now, all I had to do was wait for the results and enjoy the break.

The lockdown restrictions were easing up, giving us more freedom to step out and explore. My friends and I decided to make the most of it. We planned outings to local spots, hidden gems, and places we'd always talked about visiting but never got around to.

Each day was an adventure. We roamed around, laughed over silly things, and rediscovered the joy of simple pleasures. Our tea spot became our daily hangout again, a place where conversations flowed as freely as the chai.

Sometimes, we'd sit there for hours, reminiscing about the past, debating random topics, or just enjoying the calmness of being together. It was like reclaiming a part of life that had been on hold for so long.

During these outings, I couldn't help but think about Pari every now and then. I'd tell her about our adventures, and she'd laugh at our antics, sometimes teasing me for acting like a carefree teenager.

These moments reminded me of the balance I had found, spending time with my friends while cherishing my bond with Pari. Life felt lighter, simpler, and, for the first time in a long while, truly enjoyable.

Life had never been this good before. The days were passing by smoothly, and I was finally beginning to enjoy the little things. Then, the exam results came out.

I wasn't even interested in checking them. I was too confident about securing a management seat in the college Pari was applying to. So, I let the day pass without a second thought.

That evening, my phone rang. It was my school principal.

"How did you study for the entrance?" she asked.

I chuckled, thinking she was being sarcastic. "Honestly, ma'am, I didn't study much. With the lockdown and everything, I couldn't focus at all," I replied casually.

"Then how did you get this ranking?" she asked, her tone more serious now.

I frowned, confused. "Ranking? Ma'am, I haven't even checked the results yet," I said.

There was a brief pause before she said, "You've got a ranking of 15,000."

Her words hit me like a bolt of lightning. I was stunned.

"15,000?" I repeated, almost in disbelief.

"Yes," she confirmed.

For a moment, I couldn't speak. All I could think was how my random guessing and gut instincts during the exam had somehow worked in my favour. It was beyond belief.

The moment I heard my ranking, I ran straight to my mom.

"Mom, guess what! I got 15,000!" I blurted out, almost out of breath.

She looked at me, her expression a mix of disbelief and joy. "Are you sure?" she asked, still processing the news.

I nodded excitedly and rushed to my dad. "Dad, guess what my ranking is!"

He raised an eyebrow. "Don't tell me something ridiculous. Are you sure you entered the right registration number? Check again."

I quickly opened the results website on my phone and showed him my name and rank. "See? It's me!" I said proudly.

He stared at the screen for a moment, then shook his head with a small laugh. "You're a lucky fellow," he said.

That's when it hit me—I hadn't heard anything from Pari since the results were announced. My excitement turned into impatience. I was eager to know how she had done, and more than that, I wanted to share my surprise with her.

I picked up my phone and typed out a message: *You won't believe what happened.*

Then I waited.

Minutes turned into hours. By the time the clock struck 10 PM, there was still no reply. I figured she must have been with her parents earlier, but by now, she'd surely be done with dinner and back in her room.

My mind raced with questions. Why hadn't she replied? Did something go wrong? I debated whether to call her but decided to wait a little longer.

By 11 PM, I couldn't take it anymore. The silence was eating me alive. I picked up my phone and called her.

The first ring went unanswered. My heart sank a little. I called again, unable to stop myself.

This time, she picked up.

"Hello?" she said softly.

"Where were you? What happened? I've been worried sick!" I blurted out, the words tumbling out faster than I could think.

There was a pause on the other end.

"You didn't see my text? You weren't replying! I've been waiting for the last five hours, Pari," I said, my voice trembling slightly.

My heart was pounding, every possible scenario running through my head. Was she okay? Did something happen?

Pari's voice was low, almost a whisper. "I wasn't in the mood to talk," she said. "I got 59k ranking."

I could hear the disappointment in her tone, like a weight she was struggling to carry. "I think I'll have to go for a management seat if I want to get into a good college. But... I don't want to spend so much of my parents' money on my education," she added, her voice breaking slightly.

"It's okay, maa," I said, trying to keep my voice steady and reassuring. "You'll get into a good college, don't worry about that. And look, you can always switch branches after the first year. That way, you'll be in a good college and won't have to worry so much about spending too much."

She didn't reply immediately. I could hear her soft breathing over the phone, and I knew she was thinking about what I'd said.

"It's not just about the money," she said after a moment. "I just... I wanted to do better."

"Pari," I said gently, "you're already amazing. A ranking doesn't change that. And we'll figure this out together, okay? You're not alone in this."

After a long pause, she sighed. "Thank you, Partha. I don't know what I'd do without you."

I smiled, even though she couldn't see it. "You don't have to. I'm always here, maa."

After a moment of silence, Pari's voice broke through. "So, what was the thing you said I wouldn't believe in your text?"

I hesitated, my heart pounding. I didn't know how to tell her. She was the one who had studied, worked hard, and deserved a good rank. My rank felt like a fluke, a sheer stroke of luck. But hiding it from her wasn't an option. I couldn't lie to Pari, not about something like this.

"Well..." I began, trying to sound casual, but my voice betrayed my nervousness. "You know how I said I wasn't really studying for the entrance exams?"

"Yeah," she replied, her tone curious but calm.

"I, uh..." I paused, taking a deep breath. "I got 15k rank."

There was silence on the other end. My heart sank. Did I upset her?

"You're kidding," she said finally, her voice a mix of disbelief and something I couldn't quite place.

"I'm not," I said quickly. "I swear, I didn't expect it. I wasn't even serious about the exams. I just marked answers based on gut feeling. It's pure luck, maa. Nothing else."

She didn't respond immediately. I felt like I was holding my breath, waiting for her reaction.

"Wow," she said at last, and I couldn't tell if she was impressed, upset, or both. "You really are something, Partha."

"Pari, listen," I said earnestly. "I know you worked so hard, and you deserved a better rank. I didn't mean to"

"Stop," she interrupted, her voice soft but firm. "Don't say that. You got what you got. It's not your fault. I'm... I'm happy for you."

"You're sure?" I asked cautiously.

"Yes," she said with a small laugh. "Though, I won't lie, it's a little annoying that you did so well without studying. But that's just you, isn't it? Always surprising me."

I couldn't help but smile. "I didn't want to hurt your feelings, maa. That's the last thing I'd ever want to do."

"You didn't," she said, her tone reassuring. "I'm proud of you, Partha. Even if it's luck, you still earned it in your own way."

Her words lifted a weight off my chest. "Thanks, maa. And don't worry, we're still going to end up in the same college. No matter what."

After a pause, Pari said softly, "Partha, I'm about to tell you something, and I don't want you to feel bad about it."

I felt a lump in my throat. "What is it, maa? Just say it."

She took a deep breath. "I think you should take the college you get. You've earned a good ranking, and if we try for the same college, you'll end up in a college based on my rank. That wouldn't be fair to you."

I started to interrupt, but she continued, her voice steady but emotional. "Joining the same college might not be the best idea. It's only four years of a degree, Partha. If we try to stay together now, it might affect the next forty years of our lives. And I want those forty years to be amazing for us. You know what I mean, right?"

I was silent, listening intently as she went on.

"Our relationship started as long-distance," she reminded me. "We know how to manage it. And even if we get into different colleges, I'm sure we can handle it. Besides, my parents want me to study in the same town. I think it's better if we focus on getting into the colleges that suit us best for our own future."

Her words hit me hard, but they made sense. She wasn't saying it to push me away; she was thinking about us, about what was best for both of us in the long run.

I had nothing left to argue she was making a valid point. Still, a part of me refused to let go so easily. "Let's make it possible," I said, hoping for a different answer. But Pari had already made up her mind; she was thinking about the future, not just the present.

That was it, the dream of spending my college days with Pari was shattered. I had been just a step away from turning our long-distance relationship into something where we could finally be close, but destiny had other plans. The distance, instead of shrinking, had only grown wider. I knew it was for our future, but it still hurt. I had imagined every moment- studying together, walking through campus, sharing meals but now, those dreams faded into something that would never be.

I had once worried about how Pari would adjust to a new town, but now, that was no longer my concern. The real challenge was learning to accept this new reality.

It took us a few days to come to terms with reality. The dream of being together in the same college had slipped away, and no matter how much I tried to convince myself that it was for the best, a part of me still felt hollow. Pari and I had spent months imagining our college life together—studying in the library, sneaking out for coffee dates, walking back to our dorms after a long day. And now, all of that was gone before it even began.

We both tried to act normal, pretending that we were okay with the decision. I knew she was hurting just as much as I was, but neither of us wanted to be the one to break down first. So, we hid our sadness behind casual conversations, laughter that wasn't as genuine as before, and reassurances that felt more like unspoken apologies.

But the truth was, I didn't want to leave without seeing her one last time. I needed to look into her eyes, hold her hand, and make a memory that would stay with me during the lonely days ahead. And so, before I left for Mysuru, we decided to meet again, one final time before life pulled us in different directions.

Pari told me she would be traveling to my town again to collect some documents from our old school for her college admission. The moment I heard it, my heart felt lighter, yet at the same time, an unexplainable weight settled inside me. This was going to be our last meeting before we both moved to different cities, different colleges, and an entirely new phase of life. I knew I should be happy that we were getting this one last chance, but deep down, I was afraid.

I decided to take her to the school first and then to the same café where we had met for the first time. That café had become more than just a place for us, it was where everything had begun, where our friendship had turned into something deeper. Now, it felt like the perfect place to sit together one last time before life pulled us in different directions.

As the day of her arrival got closer, my excitement was overshadowed by an ache I couldn't shake off. I had always known that we were in a long-distance relationship, that we weren't physically together every day, but somehow, this felt different. It felt like we had been close all this time, like an invisible thread had kept us tied together, and now, for the first time, that thread was stretching too far.

I tried to push the thoughts away, telling myself that nothing would change. We would still talk every day, still share everything like we always did. But a part of me knew that once college started, once we got busy with our own lives, things wouldn't be the same. Not because we wanted them to change, but because life had a way of shifting things without asking for permission.

I didn't know how I would look into her eyes and say goodbye, knowing that after this, there would be only Just calls, messages, and the hope that distance wouldn't weaken what we had built.

I told myself to cherish every moment of this meeting, to make it count. Because once it was over, all I would have were memories—memories of us laughing over coffee, walking through the streets, stealing glances, and dreaming of a future where distance wouldn't be an issue.

And yet, no matter how much I tried to prepare myself, I knew that when the time came to say goodbye, I wouldn't be ready.

# 4

# The RED Cord...

The night before meeting Pari, I found myself restless, unable to shake off the weight of tomorrow. It wasn't just another meeting it was our last, at least for a long time. I wanted it to be perfect, something we could hold onto when the distance between us became unbearable.

So, I drove to the café, the one where we had met for the first time, the place where everything had changed. As I stepped inside, memories flooded my mind her laughter, the way she looked at me when I teased her, the way time had slipped through our fingers that day. I walked over to the exact table where we had sat before, running my fingers over its surface as if trying to capture the essence of that moment.

I found the manager and asked if I could reserve that table for the next day. He gave me a knowing smile and nodded. "Special occasion?" he asked. I just smiled back, unable to put into words how much this meant to me.

That night, I barely slept. My mind kept replaying every moment we had spent together, every call, every text, every fight, every laughter. I knew tomorrow was not the end, but it felt like a chapter closing.

The next morning, I woke up early, got dressed with more care than usual, and took my parents' car to pick Pari up. My hands gripped the steering wheel tightly as I drove, a mix of excitement and sadness swirling inside me.

When I reached the bus stop, I parked and stepped out, scanning the road for her. A few minutes later, her bus arrived. My heart pounded as I watched her step down, adjusting the strap of her bag, her eyes searching for me.

And then she started walking towards me.

In that moment, time folded in on itself. It felt exactly like the first time we had met her walking towards me, my heart racing, the world fading into the background. It was as if life had brought us full circle, back to the beginning, just to remind me how far we had come.

I smiled as she got closer, trying to hide the lump forming in my throat. This was supposed to be a happy day, a day to make memories. But deep down, I knew every step she took towards me was also a step closer to the moment we would have to say goodbye.

Pari's eyes met mine, and for a moment, everything else faded away. She smiled as she noticed the bouquet of flowers in my hand, her expression softening with a mix of surprise and amusement.

"So, you didn't forget this time?" she teased, tilting her head slightly.

I chuckled, remembering how I had forgotten to bring flowers the first time we met. "Nope, I was ready this time. That first one was just a silly mistake."

She reached out and took the bouquet, inhaling its fragrance before looking back at me. "But why did you bring the car? You know I like the scooty better."

I leaned against the car and smirked. "Well, the flowers would get spoiled in the sun, right? And besides, it's way too hot outside. I didn't want you melting before we even reached the café."

She rolled her eyes but smiled, shaking her head at my reasoning. "Always have an excuse ready, don't you?"

I opened the car door for her, and as she settled in, I stole a glance at her, trying to etch this moment into my memory. It wasn't just another meeting, it was a reminder of what we had, of what we were about to leave behind.

We had decided to go to the old school first to get the documents Pari needed, and then head to the cafe afterward. The reservation at the cafe was for a later time, so we had a bit of time before that.

Once we arrived at the school, I dropped her off at the gate, asking her to go in first. I didn't want any of my teachers to get suspicious, so I thought it would be best to keep some distance. I watched her walk inside. After a couple of minutes, I followed her inside, parked the car, and walked through the familiar hallways.

As I entered the school, I noticed that many of the teachers had changed, but a few familiar faces remained.

As I walked into the staff room, I noticed Pari talking to a few of the teachers who were still around. The familiar faces of the faculty brought back memories of the time we spent here. Suddenly, I heard a voice calling out, "Hey, aren't you Partha?" It was my Hindi teacher, who remembered me well because I had been one of the more problematic students in her class.

I smiled awkwardly and walked over to her. We started talking, and she asked, "Aren't you and Pari in the same batch?" I nodded, and she seemed genuinely happy to see us. She even mentioned how surprised she was by my entrance exam ranking, which made me feel a little proud. It was a nice feeling to have a teacher recognize the progress I had made, even though I had been a troublemaker back in the day.

After a while of chatting, my Hindi teacher told us to sit at the desk outside the clerk's office while she prepared the documents for us. Pari and I sat there quietly, our thoughts lingering on everything that had happened. The moment felt surreal, like we were in a place that had once been part of our past, but now we were about to step into the future.

I looked around at the desk where we were sitting, and a thought crossed my mind. "I think the place we were sitting is cursed," I said, half-joking but with a hint of seriousness in my voice.

"Why do you say like that?" Pari asked, a puzzled look on her face.

I took a deep breath and explained, "This was the place when I first came to know you were leaving the school and moving out of the town. And now, we're sitting here, and I'm the one leaving. Every time I sit in this place, it feels like we grow more distant."

I saw the sadness in her eyes, and my heart sank. I immediately regretted saying it out loud, but it felt like the weight of the moment was too much to ignore.

"Don't be sad, ma. It's okay, we will make it work," I said, trying to lift her spirits, even though I was struggling with my own emotions.

Pari looked at me for a moment, her eyes softening. "It feels like the same flashback is playing again in my life. That day, they were preparing your documents, and now they're preparing both of our documents," I said, my voice cracking a little. My eyes started to fill with tears, and I quickly wiped them away.

But then, Pari looked at me with such sincerity, and her voice was filled with determination. "At that time, we were not together, but this time, I am here for you. We will make it work, okay?" she said, her words like a soothing balm to my troubled heart.

Her words gave me the courage I needed. It was as if she had become my pillar, my strength. I was the one who was supposed to console her when she was down, but this time, it was her comforting me. It made me realize how much we had grown together, how much we meant to each other. Despite the distance that was coming, I knew in my heart that we would make it work.

I looked at Pari, trying to shake off the sadness that had lingered in the air. "Let's forget about everything sad and just enjoy the day. We're meeting, for God's sake! Let's make it rock!" I said, trying to sound as enthusiastic as possible, though my voice still had a slight crack from all the emotions.

Pari looked at me, her lips curling into a smile, and then she burst out laughing. "You idiot," she said, her laughter filling the air, and for a moment, it felt like everything was right again.

The sound of her laughter was like music to my ears, and it lifted my spirits in an instant. I couldn't help but smile, despite the heaviness in my heart.

Just then, our Hindi teacher came out with the documents we had been waiting for. She handed them over to us, and we both thanked her before walking out of the school. We waved at her as we made our way to the car, the familiar feeling of being with Pari making everything seem a little lighter.

We got into the car, and I started the engine, heading toward the cafe. The reservation was waiting, and this time, I promised myself we would make the most of the time we had left together. The distance between us might be growing, but for now, we were together, and that was all that mattered.

As we pulled into the cafe parking lot, Pari looked around, her eyes scanning the space. "There are so many vehicles here," she said, a hint of worry in her voice. "I think we won't get our table."

I turned to her with a reassuring smile. "Don't worry, I've reserved a table. We'll definitely get it. Come on."

Pari raised an eyebrow, clearly impressed. "Really? You do have a brain," she teased, a playful smile forming on her lips.

"Yeah, I know," I replied, trying to hide the pride in my voice.

As we walked towards the entrance, I couldn't help but joke, "After our visit, the cafe's luck had change. It's now not as empty as it was before we came."

Pari looked at me, her expression amused. "Oh, is it?" she said, teasing me back.

I grinned, feeling a warmth in my chest. Despite everything, this moment with her felt perfect. We were still together, even if only for a little while longer.

I opened the door to the cafe for her, and as she walked in, she looked at me with a smirk. "Still such a gentleman, huh?" she teased, her voice light and playful.

I couldn't help but laugh. "I try," I replied, following her inside. We made our way to the same table we had sat at the first time we met. It felt like a strange mix of nostalgia and bittersweetness. The table was just as I remembered it,small, cozy, and a little tucked away in the corner.

I ordered a coffee for myself, while Pari, looking a little hungry, ordered some pasta. As the food arrived, we settled into a comfortable rhythm, talking about everything,school, the little moments we had shared, the fun we had, and even the silly things that seemed so important at the time.

As we talked, the cafe slowly emptied out. It was just the two of us now, with only one couple sitting at a table in the far corner. The atmosphere felt calm, almost like time had slowed down for us. It was as if the world outside had faded away, and it was just the two of us in this little bubble, talking and laughing like nothing had changed.

As the cafe grew quieter, I felt the weight of my decision settle in. I had been planning this moment for days, but now that it was here, I was nervous. The idea of playing in front of Pari,my first time performing for someone,was making my heart race. But I had to do it. I couldn't let this moment slip away.

Excusing myself from the table, I told Pari I had forgotten something in the car. She nodded, a little confused, but I could see the trust in her eyes. I ran outside, my heart pounding with every step. When I reached the car, I quickly opened the trunk and grabbed my guitar. The reason I had bought the car in the first place was to hide it,so I could surprise her when the right moment came.

The night before, I had talked to the cafe manager, not only about reserving the table but also asking if I could perform there. She had agreed, but now I was second-guessing myself. When we first entered the cafe, I had planned to play, but the crowd had intimidated me. The fear of stage fright had taken over. Now, though, the cafe was almost empty,just one couple sitting in the corner and a few employees. It was the perfect moment, and if I didn't do it now, I might regret it forever.

Taking a deep breath, I walked back inside with the guitar in hand. My palms were sweaty, but I was determined. I sat back down at the table with Pari, who raised an eyebrow at the guitar. "What's that for?" she asked, a playful grin tugging at her lips.

I smiled, trying to calm my nerves. "I thought I'd play something for you," I said, my voice a little shakier than I intended. "If you don't mind."

Her eyes widened, and I could see the surprise and excitement in them. "You're going to play for me? Now?"

I nodded, my hands trembling as I adjusted the guitar. "Yeah," I said, "I've been wanting to do this for a while."

As I strummed the first chord, the sound of the guitar filled the air. The nervousness melted away with each note, and slowly, I lost myself in the music. It wasn't perfect, but it didn't matter. I was playing for her, and that was all that counted.

I could feel her eyes on me, and when I glanced up, I saw her smiling softly, her gaze filled with warmth and affection. It made everything worth it. The nerves, the hesitation,it all faded away. This moment was ours, and nothing else mattered.

As I started playing *Photograph* by Ed Sheeran, the familiar melody flowed from my fingers, and I began to sing, pouring all my emotions into each word. The moment felt surreal,just me, my guitar, and Pari, with the soft hum of the cafe surrounding us. But as I continued, I noticed something out of the corner of my eye. The couple at the other table had stood up and walked over to us. The employees, too, gathered near our table, intrigued by the song.

I felt a wave of nervousness wash over me. The attention was overwhelming, but all I could focus on was Pari. I wanted this to be perfect for her, to create a memory that would stay with her forever. I tried to block out the growing crowd and just kept singing, hoping that my voice could convey what words alone couldn't.

As I finished the last line, the cafe erupted into applause. The couple from the other table clapped enthusiastically, and one of them patted me on the back. "You sung good," he said with a smile.

I turned my gaze to Pari, my heart pounding in my chest. I saw her sitting there, her eyes glistening with tears. It hit me all at once, the overwhelming emotion, the love we shared, and the fact that I had just done something for her that I'd always wanted to do.

Before I could even process it, she stood up, walked toward me, and without saying a word, wrapped her arms around me in the tightest hug. I could feel her trembling, her face pressed against my chest.

"I never felt so loved, Partha," she whispered, her voice thick with emotion. "Thank you... it was beautiful."

In that moment, everything else faded away. The cafe, the people, the world outside,it all disappeared. It was just me and Pari, and for once, everything felt right.

Now I knew I had made her happy. That was all I wanted, to give her a moment she would never forget.

After wiping the tears from her eyes, Pari looked at me and asked, "When did you learn to play the guitar?" Her voice was still shaky, but a smile tugged at her lips.

I chuckled, looking down at my guitar. "I was practicing during the lockdown," I admitted. "I wanted to surprise you when we went to college together... but that won't happen now. So, I thought, why not play it today?"

She stared at me for a moment, her expression unreadable. Then, she shook her head with a soft laugh. "You're such an idiot," she whispered, but I could see the love in her eyes.

And in that moment, I didn't care about anything else. Not the distance that would soon separate us, not the uncertainty of the future just the fact that I had made her happy today.

After the café, I had planned to watch the sunset with her, but we still had some time to spare. So, we decided to go for a short ride outside the city,just to enjoy the moment a little longer. The wind was cool, and the roads were quiet, making it the perfect escape.

The whole ride, Pari wouldn't stop teasing me. "What if you got nervous and missed the lyrics? Or what if you messed up the chords? Wouldn't that have been embarrassing?" she asked, grinning.

I smirked. "Even if I missed a chord or forgot the lyrics, you wouldn't have noticed because you were too busy being surprised and crying, right?"

She gasped dramatically, then burst into laughter. I joined her, the sound of our laughter blending with the hum of the engine and the rustling wind.

For that brief ride, everything felt perfect,like we had frozen time, just the two of us, away from all the worries of the future.

As the sun dipped lower into the horizon, we made our way back to the riverbank,the same place I had taken her the first time we met. The air was cool, and the golden glow of the setting sun reflected off the water, making everything feel surreal.

Pari climbed onto the bonnet of the car, her legs swinging gently, while I leaned against it, facing her. The silence between us was comfortable, the kind where words weren't needed. Yet, when I turned to look at her, I found her already looking at me.

"What, maa?" I asked, smiling.

"Nothing," she replied softly, her eyes lingering on me a little longer.

I looked back at the horizon and spoke, my voice calm but firm. "Even though the sun is setting, it's still beautiful. We know darkness is coming, but that doesn't stop us from enjoying the sunset." I turned back to her. "Just like our relationship. The distance might feel like darkness, but the sun always rises again. And so will we. We just have to get through this night." I paused, watching as a single tear welled up in her eyes. "Besides, the night isn't even that bad... we have the moon."

Pari was speechless. She simply stared at me, processing my words. Then, with tears glistening in her eyes and a huge smile on her face, she finally whispered, "Yes, Partha. We will rise again."

After the sunset, it was finally time for her to go home. We got into the car, but the air inside felt heavy. Neither of us spoke. We both knew that once this drive ended, the distance between us would truly begin.

As I reached for the keys to start the car, Pari suddenly leaned toward me and wrapped her arms around me in a tight hug. Her warmth made my chest feel heavier, but at the same time, it was comforting.

When she pulled away, she reached into her bag and took out a small brown packet.

"What is it, maa?" I asked, curiosity filling my voice.

She didn't answer right away. Instead, she carefully unwrapped it and took out a delicate red cord.

I frowned slightly. "What's this?"

Her eyes sparkled with excitement as she explained, "I read about this... According to a Japanese legend, two soulmates are connected by a red thread tied by the gods. The thread may tangle, it may stretch, but it will never break. No matter how far apart they are, it will always find its way back." She looked up at me, her eyes full of certainty. "Just like us. Right now, our thread is stretching, getting tangled... but we'll always find our way back."

I was speechless. A wave of emotions crashed over me, but I forced myself to hold them back. I didn't want to break down in front of her, not now. Instead, I managed a small smile and said, "Is that so?"

Pari took my wrist gently and tied the red cord around it, her fingers lingering on my skin for a second longer. Then she held out the other piece, "Now, tie this around my wrist."

With slightly trembling hands, I did as she asked, securing the red thread around her wrist.

"Thank you, maa. This is such a beautiful gift," I whispered, my voice barely steady.

Pari just smiled. "Now, no matter where we go, we'll always be connected."

I started the car and drove toward the bus stand. The silence between us was deafening, but neither of us dared to break it. We both knew that if we spoke, even a single word, the dam holding back our emotions would burst.

As we reached the bus stand, her bus was already there, waiting. I pulled over and parked. "That's it for today," I said, trying to sound casual, but my voice betrayed me.

I turned to look at her. Pari's eyes held a sadness so deep that it hurt to see. She didn't say anything,she just leaned in and hugged me tightly, as if she was trying to take all of me in before she left. As she pulled away, she ruffled my hair, giving me a head rub.

I frowned, trying to lighten the mood. "Why the head rub? Am I a dog?"

She let out a small chuckle, her voice barely above a whisper. "No, you're an idiot."

We got out of the car, and I walked her to the bus. As she climbed in and took her seat, I stood outside, not moving, just looking at her. She turned toward me, our eyes meeting one last time through the window. She didn't wave, didn't smile just looked, as if trying to memorize my face.

As the bus pulled away, I still stood there, watching until it faded into the distance. But that wasn't enough I got into my car and quietly followed the bus for a while, making sure she was safe, making sure she was still close, even if she didn't know it.

Eventually, I had to stop. I watched the taillights disappear into the night, and with a heavy heart, I turned back, driving home with nothing but the red thread around my wrist and the ache of distance settling in.

Two hours later, my phone lit up with a message from Pari: "Reached home."

A wave of relief washed over me. I had been tense about her traveling alone, but now I could finally breathe easy.

That night, I called her. The moment she picked up, I tried to lighten the mood. "So, how was your date? I heard you went out with the most handsome guy in town today."

Pari scoffed. "Noo, he's an idiot. I just went out with him out of pity," she replied sarcastically.

"Really?" I asked, playing along.

She paused for a second and then said, "No, Partha... you're cute."

I felt my face heat up. Before I could even enjoy the compliment, she added with a teasing laugh, "But don't be too happy, you're not *that* cute."

We both burst out laughing.

After a moment, her voice softened. "I already miss you..."

I sighed. "It's okay, maa. We can talk every day, and I promise,I'll call you every night. And at least *one* video call every day. Deal?"

"Deal," she whispered.

And just like that, even with miles between us, we still felt close.

That night, we both fell asleep quickly, exhausted from all the traveling and emotions of the day.

The next morning, I woke up early, ready to shop for everything I needed for my hostel in Mysuru. It was an exciting yet bittersweet day. I had already visited Mysuru before and loved the city,the vibrant streets, the pleasant weather, and the overall atmosphere. I felt lucky to get a college there.

But the one thing missing was **Pari.**

No matter how much I looked forward to this new chapter, a part of me wished she was coming along too.

Things between me and Pari were going really well. In fact, she also got admission to a good engineering college near her home, not just any college, but one she got into through the entrance exam results. It was a relief for both of us.

Even though college was about to start, I was still at home, preparing for my move to Mysuru. There were so many things to pack, and the reality of leaving was slowly sinking in. Pari, on the other hand, had even more on her plate. Her parents had built a new house, and the housewarming function was coming up, keeping her occupied.

But no matter how hectic things got, we still made time for each other. Every day, no matter what, we talked. Some days, it was for hours; other days, just a few messages. But we never let a day pass without hearing from each other.

After a week, I had some work in Pari's town, and the moment I found out, I was beyond excited. We had both thought we wouldn't be able to meet anytime soon, but now, out of nowhere, we were getting a chance to see each other again.

That day, I went to Pari's home. Her parents had known me since childhood, so they were thrilled to see me after so many years. They welcomed me warmly and offered me coffee as we sat down to talk. It felt nostalgic, sitting in their home, reminiscing about old days.

While I was engaged in conversation with her parents, Pari couldn't resist teasing me. From the corner of my eye, I could see her giving me side glances, playfully smirking. Whenever her parents turned their backs, she'd act like she was blowing me a flying kiss, and I, trying to keep a straight face, pretended to catch it. It was a silent game between us, one that made my heart race and my face light up with a stupid grin.

Even in a room full of people, it felt like it was just the two of us, lost in our own little world.

After a while, we decided to visit Pari's new house. As we were getting ready to leave, her dad suddenly asked me to stay over for the night. I wanted to,I really did but I had some important work back home, so I had to politely decline.

Pari's dad had some errands to run, so he left, and it was just me, Pari, and her mom heading to their new house. When we arrived, the place was already taking shape, but there were still a few final touches left some interior work, a bit of painting, and a few furniture pieces yet to be arranged.

Pari was excited, showing me around like a little kid, explaining how she had helped pick out certain designs, arguing with her parents over colour choices, and envisioning how the house would look once it was fully ready. I could see the happiness in her eyes this place wasn't just a house; it was her home, the one she had always dreamed of.

I couldn't help but admire her as she excitedly pointed out every little detail. This was a new beginning for her, and I was just grateful to be there, witnessing it.

As we went upstairs to check out Pari's room, her mom stayed downstairs, inspecting the woodwork that was still in progress. Pari eagerly led the way, excited to show me the space that would soon become her own.

The moment I stepped inside, I suddenly felt a force from behind a pair of warm arms wrapping around me tightly. It was Pari. She hugged me from behind, pressing her face against my back. I froze for a second, feeling the warmth of her embrace, the way she held me as if she never wanted to let go.

Then, in a soft whisper, she said, "I wanted to hug you for so long. I was controlling myself because my parents were there."

I turned slightly to look at her, chuckling. There she was, holding onto me as if the world would pull us apart at any second. In that moment, I knew without a doubt that she loved me just as much as I loved her. We both wanted the same thing: to be together, always.

After a minute, she still didn't loosen her grip. I laughed and said, "It's okay, maa. Let me go, or my intestines and liver will spill out if you hold me any tighter."

Pari giggled but finally unwrapped her arms. Just as I thought she was letting go completely, she leaned in and placed a soft kiss on my cheek before stepping back. My heart skipped a beat, but before I could react, she grabbed my hand and pulled me towards the stairs.

As we reached downstairs, her mom looked at us and asked, "So, how was it?" She was referring to the room, of course.

I glanced at Pari with a smirk and replied, "It was too good. I felt nice."

Pari caught the hidden meaning behind my words, her cheeks turning a slight shade of pink as she nudged me playfully.

After a while, it was finally time to leave. I glanced at Pari, and I could see the change in her expression. The charm, the excitement that had been there all morning, had faded. She wasn't saying anything, but her face said it all.

Her mom was still there, so I couldn't say much aloud. Instead, I took out my phone and quickly typed a message:

"It's okay, maa. We'll talk soon, okay? I really have to go now. Don't be sad if you are, I won't be able to leave. I'll feel sad too."

I sent the text and then looked at her, subtly signalling with my eyes to check her phone.

Pari looked at her phone, read my text, and then lifted her gaze to meet mine. She smiled, not her usual, bright, carefree smile, but one filled with warmth, a smile meant to reassure me even though I knew she was just trying to make me feel better.

I turned to her mom, took her blessings, and then waved goodbye to Pari. She waved back, her eyes holding onto mine for a moment longer than usual. Then, with a heavy heart, I got into my car and started driving home.

As I pulled away, I could see Pari standing near the gate, watching my car as it moved further and further away. She didn't move, didn't wave again just stood there, looking, as if trying to make the moment last a little longer. I glanced at the rearview mirror, catching one last glimpse of her before I turned the corner and disappeared from her sight.

I wanted to stop. I wanted to run back and hold her one last time. But I knew if I did, leaving would become even more painful. So, I kept driving, letting the distance grow, even though every part of me wished it wouldn't.

As I drove a little farther from her home, a notification popped up on the car's display screen. It was a message from Pari:

*"Thank you for coming, maa. I really needed to see you. I was too stressed from all this work, but today I felt kind of relaxed."*

I chuckled softly, reading her words. I could almost hear her voice saying them. I wanted to reply immediately, to tell her that I felt the same, that seeing her made everything feel lighter. But I knew better. If I replied now, she'd know for sure that I was texting while driving, and she would definitely scold me.

So instead, I just smiled to myself, gripping the steering wheel a little tighter, my heart feeling just a little warmer.

After a while, I finally reached home and texted Pari:

*"I reached home, maa. And honestly, I felt the same way you did. Today was really special."*

She replied instantly with a heart emoji, and I smiled as I put my phone away.

I handed over the documents to my dad and freshened up before heading out to meet my friends. It had been a while since we all sat together at our usual spot for tea. As I reached there, I called everyone to catch up. Mithun and Pratham were the first to arrive.

As soon as Mithun sat down next to me, he sniffed the air and asked, "What perfume are you wearing? Smells like something floral."

I was confused for a second, then it hit me I wasn't wearing any perfume. It was Pari's scent, still lingering on my shirt from when she hugged me so tightly. I hadn't even noticed it over the smell of the car's air freshener.

I quickly played it cool. "Uh... must be from some fabric freshener or something," I said casually, avoiding eye contact. There was no way I was telling them I had gone to meet Pari.

A few minutes later, Sai, Anni, Jai, Swasthik, Siddu, and Roopal also joined. We sat there, talking and laughing for over an hour, catching up on everything we had missed in each other's lives. It felt good to be with them again, just like old times.

After a while, as the evening set in, we all said our goodbyes and headed back home.

After dinner, I lay on my bed when Pari's call popped up. We started talking about the day, laughing about how we both tried to act normal around her parents. She teased me about almost giving us away when her mom asked about the rooms, and I reminded her how she kept messing with me behind their backs.

We talked for hours about college, how much we already missed each other, and how she wished I could've stayed longer. I reassured her that we'd meet again soon and promised to talk every day. Eventually, we both drifted off to sleep, still on the call.

As the days passed and my move to the new town got closer, Pari and I started missing each other even more. I was stressed about leaving, and she was overwhelmed with the housewarming preparations. The calls and texts weren't enough we were desperate to meet again.

Then one evening, Pari came up with a plan.

Pari had planned to visit my town with her parents to distribute invitations for their housewarming ceremony. It was the perfect excuse for us to meet again, and we were both excited about it. However, on the day of the trip, her father fell slightly ill, and they had to cancel their plans.

Despite this setback, Pari was determined not to let this opportunity slip away. She decided to take matters into her own hands, volunteering to distribute the invitations by herself. It wasn't just about the invitations deep down, I knew she was doing this just so she could see me one more time before I left for college. Her determination made me smile, and I couldn't wait for the moment we'd meet again.

I was just as excited as she was. I assured her that I would help her in any way I could and make things easier for her. With everything set in motion, the plan worked perfectly she arrived in my town, and we got to spend the entire day together.

I became her designated driver, taking her from one relative's house to another, as well as stopping by her neighbour's places to hand out the invitations. Though the task itself was tiring, neither of us minded. What truly mattered was that we had found a way to be together, even if just for a little longer.

Three days later, I got the news that my college would be starting within a week. At first, I didn't think much of it, just another step toward my future. But then, like a slow, sinking weight in my chest, the realization hit me. I wouldn't be able to attend Pari's housewarming function.

I sat there for a while, staring at my phone, trying to figure out how to break it to her. I knew how much this meant to her. It wasn't just about moving into a new house;

it was about creating a home, a place where she had envisioned us sharing countless memories. And now, I wouldn't be there for it.

When I finally told her, there was a long silence on the other end. I could almost hear her processing the words, the quiet disappointment settling in. "Oh..." she finally whispered. Just that one word, but I could feel the sadness wrapped around it.

I hated it. I hated the fact that I was letting her down, even if it wasn't in my control. I wanted to be there, to stand beside her as she welcomed people into her new home, to see her eyes light up with excitement, to be part of this new beginning. But now, all of that was slipping through my fingers.

Sensing my guilt, Pari quickly pulled herself together. "It's okay," she said, her voice suddenly light, as if trying to mask her emotions. "College is important, Partha. I get it. You have to go."

I could hear the forced smile in her voice, the way she was trying to convince not just me, but herself too.

"I'll send you all the photos," she continued, her tone turning playful, as if that could somehow make up for the emptiness I felt. "I'll make sure you don't miss anything. And after it's over, I'll tell you every single detail, down to what colour saree my mom wore and which uncle complained about the food. That way, we'll have a whole week's worth of things to talk about at night."

I let out a small chuckle at her attempt to make me feel better, but deep down, I knew she was just as upset as I was. She had been looking forward to this day, picturing it with me by her side. And now, that picture had changed.

"I'm really sorry, Maa..." I said softly.

She was quiet for a moment before whispering, "Me too."

I wished I could tell her that I'd find a way, that I'd show up at her doorstep on the day of the function and surprise her. But reality was cruel, and the truth was, there was nothing I could do.

As we ended the call that night, a heavy silence settled over me. We were both trying to be strong for each other, but the distance was already making its presence known. And for the first time, I truly felt just how far apart we were going to be.

# 5

## Keeping the Flame Alive...

Finally, the day arrived. My college started, and I had to leave my hometown. It felt surreal, like stepping into a new chapter of my life while leaving behind a part of myself. The dream that Pari and I had of studying in the same college, walking the same corridors, sharing the same experiences was now just that, a dream. It wasn't possible anymore.

I did have a chance to secure a management seat at her college, but Pari had insisted otherwise. "It's not about just being together, Partha," she had told me. "You need to go where you truly belong, where you'll grow. We'll find our way back to each other no matter what." She had said it with so much confidence, so much certainty, but now, as I stood in an unfamiliar city, I felt the weight of our distance more than ever.

The first day at college was a mix of emotions. There was excitement this was something new, a fresh start. There was also fear being in a new city, meeting new people, trying to fit in. And then there was the undeniable sadness because Pari wasn't with me. She should've been walking beside me, teasing me about how nervous I was, making fun of my serious expressions. But instead, we were miles apart, living separate experiences.

I tried to focus, to take in everything around me, but my mind kept wandering back to her. Would she be thinking about me right now? Was she missing me as much as I missed her?

The first day of college passed in a blur. I barely got the chance to talk to anyone just a few casual introductions, nothing more. Everything felt new, yet strangely distant, like I was watching myself go through the motions rather than actually living them.

When the day ended, I returned to my college hostel. It was impressive spacious, well-equipped, almost luxurious compared to what I had expected. But no matter how comfortable it was, it wasn't home. It had all the facilities, but none of the warmth. The silence in the room felt heavier than usual, maybe because I wasn't used to ending my day without seeing familiar faces or hearing voices that felt like home.

That first night, I was alone in my room. The space around me felt foreign, uninviting. The only sign of life was coming from the room next door, where three students had already settled in. One of them was Karthik, he was in the same branch as me, studying Information Science, but in a different section. The other two were from different branches altogether. I could hear their muffled laughter through the walls, a reminder that I was yet to find my place here.

Lying on my bed, staring at the unfamiliar ceiling, I felt the weight of the distance between me and everything I had known. The excitement of a new beginning was there, but so was the quiet ache of leaving something precious behind.

That night felt even lonelier because I couldn't even talk to Pari. She had a ceremony at home, and I knew she'd be busy, surrounded by family and guests. I wanted to text her, just a simple *I miss you*, but I didn't want to disturb her. So, I just sat in my room, staring at my phone, scrolling mindlessly, feeling the weight of the silence around me.

Just then, Karthik from the next room walked in. He introduced himself with an easy-going smile, and I shook his hand, telling him my name. He didn't wait for an invitation; he just casually leaned against the doorframe and started talking. There was something comforting about the way he spoke, like he had already adjusted to this place while I was still struggling to.

After a few minutes, he invited me to his room to meet his roommates. I hesitated for a second stepping into a room full of strangers wasn't exactly what I had planned for the night. But then again, sitting alone wasn't making me feel any better either. So, I followed him.

His roommates were welcoming, cracking jokes and making it easy for me to join the conversation. For the first time that day, I felt a little less like an outsider. When it was time for dinner, we all went together, and I realized how much I needed that moment to sit with people, to share a meal, to laugh even if my heart wasn't completely in it yet.

That night, as I returned to my room, I felt a little lighter. Maybe this place wouldn't feel like home just yet, but at least I wasn't entirely alone.

Late that night, around 2 AM, my phone lit up with a message notification. *You up?*

It was from Pari.

I wasn't deep into sleep anyway. It was a new place, a new bed, and no matter how tired I was, my mind just wouldn't shut off. I had been staring at the ceiling, lost in thoughts, when her message brought me back. Without hesitation, I grabbed my phone and replied, *Yupppp.*

*I'm sorry,* she texted back almost instantly. *I was too busy with the ceremony. How was your day?*

I sighed, thinking about it for a second before typing, *it was okay-ish. Made a friend in the next hostel room, Karthik. He seems chill. But at college, it was just casual greetings so far. Still need someone who matches my vibe. The hostel is fine, I guess... just doesn't feel like home yet.*

I stared at the screen, waiting for her response, feeling a little lighter just from sharing that. I knew she'd say something to make me feel better. She always did

Pari's reply came almost immediately.

*"It's okay if it doesn't feel like home on the first day. You'll gradually settle in. It's always difficult at first. But from tomorrow onwards, I'll be with you every time you need me. You can call me anytime, right? Just adjust for a day or two, okay?"*

I read her words and exhaled slowly. She always knew exactly what to say. Even through a screen, she made me feel like I wasn't alone. I could almost hear her voice in my head, soft yet reassuring.

I smiled to myself and replied, *Yeah, I know. Just feels weird without you here. But I'll be fine. Thanks, Maa.*

She sent a heart emoji, and that was enough. Even though she wasn't physically here, she still found a way to make me feel at home.

Then I quickly replied, "Now go to sleep, or you'll look tired in all the housewarming pictures. You're not that good-looking anyway if you're tired, you'll look even worse." I teased her.

Almost immediately, my phone buzzed with an angry emoji as a response. I laughed, knowing she'd be fuming on the other end.

I quickly followed up, "You're the cutest one... except me. You look good, Maa, I was just teasing you a little."

Her reply came back just as fast, "Yet, you're still teasing a little in that reply too!"

I could almost hear the annoyed tone in her voice, but deep down, I knew she was smiling.

Then I texted her, "Good night, Maa."

Even though we had talked for only ten minutes, I felt a sense of complete satisfaction. A wave of relief washed over me something I couldn't quite put into words. The unfamiliar walls of my hostel room, which had felt cold and distant just moments ago, now didn't seem so strange anymore.

That's when I realized—**home isn't a place. It's a feeling**. And for me, home was wherever Pari was.

Then I remembered an article I had read a few days ago. It said that all you need is just **eight minutes** with your loved ones to not feel alone. At that moment, I realized how true it was.

Just a short conversation, even a simple check-in, could make such a huge difference. Loneliness had a way of creeping in, making everything seem heavier than it really was. But talking to someone even just a friend could shift everything. It was in these small moments that I understood how people sometimes made bad decisions when they felt isolated.

A single conversation, a single voice that cared, could change everything.

The next day, I woke up and went to college. Slowly, I started settling in l made some new friends in class, and for the first time, I felt like I was beginning to fit into this new city. The day passed quickly, keeping me occupied, but once again, I didn't get the chance to talk to Pari.

Later that night, around 2:30 AM, a notification popped up on my phone. It was Pari.

*"You up?"*

I replied instantly, knowing well that she would scold me for not sleeping. And she did. I smirked as I read her texts, but I threw it right back at her. *"You should be sleeping too,"* I texted.

*"I have so many stories to tell you about the function!"* she replied excitedly.

I could almost hear the enthusiasm in her voice, imagine the sparkle in her eyes as she spoke, and the way she would get animated while telling every little detail. That thought itself made me excited. There was something about hearing her talk her voice, her expressions, the way she made even the simplest things feel special.

I was just waiting for the next day to arrive because, from then on, Pari would always be available to talk, and I wouldn't feel as lonely as I did now. That thought kept me going, making me look forward to something comforting amidst all the changes around me.

The next day, I went to college as usual, and to my surprise, I started blending in better. I made even more friends, and soon, we had formed a group of twelve. What made our group special was that we weren't just from one section four students from three different sections had come together, which was rare. Since we all had the same break time, the cafeteria became our go-to spot, where we would gather, talk, and laugh.

For the first time since arriving in this new city, I felt like I belonged somewhere. The feeling of loneliness that had weighed on me since the day I left home was slowly fading.

Later that evening, around 7 PM, I got a call from Pari. The moment I picked up, it felt like all the distance between us disappeared. We talked for hours—three, maybe four—completely lost in our conversation. She told me every little detail about the housewarming function, how things went, who came, what funny moments happened, and how she felt throughout the day. The way she narrated everything, with her usual excitement and those little dramatic pauses, made me feel like I had been there with her.

Time slipped away so fast that we even forgot about dinner. It was only around 11 PM when I realized we had been talking nonstop. Wanting to show her a bit of my world, I casually asked Pari to switch the voice call to a video call. The moment the screen lit up with her face, I felt a strange sense of comfort. I turned my camera around to show her my hostel room, giving her a little tour of my space, and she teased me about how plain and boring it looked.

From there, our conversation just flowed naturally. We talked about anything and everything our day, our plans, silly jokes, and things that didn't even matter but felt so important in the moment. Before we knew it, it was already 2 AM. It was only then that I realized something I had completely forgotten that I was in a new city, a new place, surrounded by unfamiliar people. Talking to Pari made me feel like I was home.

The days seemed to slip by like sand through my fingers. Life at college was slowly becoming more manageable. I had made a small group of friends, people who made the unfamiliar city feel a little less daunting. Pari, too, was finding her rhythm in her new college, making friends and settling into her own routine. Though our lives were moving in different directions, our bond remained as strong as ever.

It had been two months since college started, and I began to long for home. The thought of being back in the comforting familiarity of my hometown filled me with excitement. So, I decided to plan a trip home, knowing it would recharge me. Naturally, the first thing I did was ask Pari if we could meet. After all, the thought of seeing her again was always the highlight of any plan I made.

But this time, it was not meant to be. Pari had her internals scheduled during the same week, and she couldn't afford to take a break. I could hear the disappointment in her voice when she told me, "I really wish I could, but I can't miss my internals. They're too important." I tried to sound understanding, reassuring her that it was okay, even though my heart ached a little.

It was in moments like these that I realized just how far we had come in our relationship. Distance wasn't a hurdle for us anymore; it was just another challenge we navigated together. The love and connection we shared didn't waver, even if we couldn't physically be together. Every evening, we would talk on video calls, sharing every detail of our days. We laughed, teased, and comforted each other as if the miles between us didn't exist.

Pari would often narrate stories about her college, her new friends, and the little things that made her day. I would do the same, telling her about my experiences, my classes, and the random mischief my friends and I got into. It felt as though we were living each other's lives, piece by piece, through those conversations.

Though I couldn't see her in person this time, I knew one thing for sure: no matter the distance, no matter how busy life got, we would always find a way back to each other. In a way, our relationship had become a safe haven a constant in an ever-changing world.

That weekend at home was exactly what I needed a comforting escape from the hustle of the new city and college life. I hadn't told my parents I was coming, so the look of surprise on their faces when I walked through the door was priceless. My mom, in her usual way, scolded me for not informing them earlier, but I could tell how happy she was. My dad, always calm and composed, gave me a warm smile, his eyes saying everything words couldn't.

The familiar aroma of home-cooked food, the laughter that echoed through the house, and the simple joy of sitting with my family at the dinner table made me realize how much I missed home. That weekend, I reconnected with some of my old friends who had also returned home from their colleges. It felt like the old days, carefree and full of laughter, as if nothing had changed. We talked about our new lives, our colleges, and all the experiences we had gathered over the past few months. It was refreshing to sit in our favourite spots and reminisce about the times when life was simpler.

But just as quickly as it started, the weekend came to an end. Time, as always, seemed to move too fast when I was home. And before I knew it, it was time to pack my bags and leave again. As I hugged my mom goodbye, I noticed the subtle sadness in her eyes, though she didn't say a word. My dad patted my shoulder and told me to take care of myself, his voice steady but softer than usual.

As the car left the city, an ache settled in my chest a heaviness that I couldn't shake. Looking out at the familiar streets and landmarks, I felt a lump form in my throat. It was the same city I had grown up in, the same streets where I had made countless memories, and now, every time I left, it felt like I was leaving a piece of myself behind.

But I knew this was something I had to do a necessary step toward building my future. It didn't make it any easier, though. The ache lingered as the city grew smaller in the rearview mirror. All I could do was hold on to the memories of the weekend and remind myself that, no matter how far I went, home would always be there, waiting for me.

Now, as the college routine resumed, life fell back into its structured rhythm. But this time, I decided to shake things up a bit. I didn't want to just go through the motions of classes, assignments, and hostel life. I wanted to feel alive, to reignite the spark I had as a child when I was always so active and curious.

So, I took the first step toward that by signing up for guitar lessons again. It had been years since I last strummed a chord, but I still remembered the joy and calm it brought me. Picking up the guitar again felt like reconnecting with an old friend, and though my fingers were a bit rusty, the music slowly started to flow. Each evening, after classes, I'd spend time practicing, sometimes losing track of time. The sound of the strings filled my otherwise quiet hostel room, and for the first time, it felt a little less empty.

But that wasn't enough for me. I wanted to explore more and push myself out of my comfort zone. When I heard about an inter-college tech competition, I didn't hesitate to sign up. It was a chance to challenge myself, to work on something creative and innovative. The process was intense, with brainstorming sessions, late-night preparations, and endless discussions with my teammates. But I loved every second of it. It reminded me of the little competitions I used to participate in back home during school days, the thrill of putting in the effort and the excitement of being part of something bigger.

When I found out that I had been selected to represent my college, I couldn't believe it. It was a proud moment, not just for me but also for the friends and teachers who had encouraged me to step up. It felt like I was slowly rediscovering myself, piece by piece, in this new city, away from the comfort of home and familiarity.

These activities didn't just keep me occupied they gave me a sense of purpose. They helped me feel more connected to my college life, to the people around me, and to myself. It was as if, amidst the chaos of adapting to a new place, I was carving out my own little space, one string, one idea, and one step at a time.

Moving out of the hostel and into a rented house was a game-changer for me. The strict hostel curfew at 8 PM had become a constant source of frustration, especially since my guitar classes ended at the same time. Every night, I had to call my parents and convince the warden about why I was late, which was exhausting. On top of that, my friends from the next room in the hostel had already moved out to rented places and kept raving about the freedom they were enjoying. That's when I decided it was time to make the move.

I talked to Karthik, my next-room neighbour and one of my closest friends. We had hit it off during our hostel days, and living together seemed like a natural choice. After nearly two weeks of searching, dealing with brokers, and inspecting houses, we finally found a cozy 2BHK apartment not too far from college. It felt like the perfect place to start this new chapter.

The freedom of having our own place was exhilarating. Suddenly, the city that once felt strange started feeling more welcoming. But with freedom came responsibility cooking, cleaning, and managing the house. Luckily, I already knew how to cook, so it wasn't as daunting as it could have been. In fact, cooking turned into a bonding activity. On weekends, my friends would show up with a packet of chicken, and I'd prepare lunch for everyone. We'd gather around, eat, laugh, and talk for hours. Those moments became traditions that brought us closer together.

Before long, our house became the unofficial hangout spot. Mithun, who still lived in the hostel, would often spend the night at our place. Amruth, staying in a PG, and Rohith, who lived nearby, also became regular visitors. The evenings were always lively. We'd play card games or carrom late into the night, filling the house with laughter and energy.

What used to be casual meetups in the college cafeteria now shifted to our living room. Sitting together with snacks and chai, we'd talk about everything college, life, and the dreams we were all chasing. It was messy and chaotic at times, but it was also perfect in its own way.

This move didn't just bring freedom, it brought a sense of community, responsibility, and belonging. It turned what initially felt like a lonely, unfamiliar city into a place I could truly call home. For the first time, life felt less like a routine and more like an adventure, surrounded by friends who made every moment worthwhile.

Even as I was making new friends in college and settling into this new chapter of my life, I never forgot my old friends. Staying connected with them was important to me because they had been such a big part of my journey. I made it a point to call them regularly, sharing updates about my life and checking in on theirs.

I called Sowmika every day, especially because I knew she was struggling to adjust to her new college. She was having a hard time settling in, and I wanted to be there for her, just like she had always been for me. Those daily calls became our way of keeping each other grounded. Sometimes, I would just listen to her vent about her day, and other times, I'd try to cheer her up with random stories or jokes. It felt good to be able to support her even from a distance.

Advaya, on the other hand, was a completely different story. She was an extrovert, full of energy and always eager to share every little detail about her life. She seemed to thrive in her new college environment, quickly making friends and getting involved in various activities. Her excitement was infectious, and whenever I visited her usually once every couple of months, we'd spend the entire day talking, laughing, and exploring her city.

She had a way of making every visit feel like an adventure, whether it was taking me to her favourite hangout spots, introducing me to her new friends, or just reminiscing about our shared memories. Her vibrant personality reminded me to embrace life with enthusiasm, and I always left those visits feeling recharged and inspired.

Even with all the new experiences, late-night hangouts, and the excitement of college life, keeping my bond with my old friends alive felt like anchoring myself to my roots. They were my constants, and no matter how far I went or how many new connections I made, they were always going to be a part of my life. Balancing these relationships wasn't always easy, but it was worth every effort. It reminded me that friendships, old or new, are what truly keep us grounded.

As the days passed, something truly exciting happened. I got selected to participate in a competition that was being held at Pari's college. The moment I heard the news, I couldn't contain my excitement. I was practically jumping with joy, my heart racing at the thought of seeing Pari after so long. My teammates, seeing me so ecstatic, naturally assumed I was just thrilled about the competition itself. Little did they know, the real reason behind my happiness had nothing to do with the competition, it was all about getting the chance to see Pari.

They didn't know about me and Pari, and I had no intention of spilling the beans just yet. Instead, I quietly stepped outside, pulled out my phone, and instinctively dialled Pari's number. Just as the call connected, I realized it might have been better to surprise her instead. But before I could hang up, Pari picked up the call.

"Hello?" she said. Her familiar, sweet voice made my heart skip a beat.

"Hey!" I replied, unable to hide the excitement in my tone.

"Whoa, what is it? You sound so happy!" Pari asked curiously, her voice tinged with warmth and curiosity.

"Nothing, I'm just... casual," I replied, trying my best to sound nonchalant.

"No, there's definitely something in your voice," Pari pressed, her intuition sharper than ever. "You sound different."

I couldn't help but smile. It was moments like these that reminded me how deeply Pari knew me, how effortlessly she could pick up on the slightest changes in my mood. I felt so touched, so seen, but I still didn't want to spoil the surprise.

"It's nothing, really," I said, trying to sound as convincing as possible. "I just... wanted to talk to you, that's it."

"Okay..." Pari said slowly, her tone laced with confusion and a hint of suspicion. She didn't seem entirely convinced, but she didn't push further.

Hanging up, I felt a mix of guilt and excitement. I knew she'd probably dwell on that brief conversation, wondering what had me so giddy. But I also knew the look on her face when she saw me at her college would make it all worth it. The thought of her surprise and happiness fueled me even more. Now, I just had to wait for the day of the competition to finally reunite with her—and I couldn't wait.

The day before the competition, we had to board a train late at night. I knew I had to keep my plan intact, so earlier that evening, I called Pari, pretending to have a slight headache. "I'm feeling a bit under the weather, ma. I think I'll sleep early tonight," I said, doing my best to sound convincing. Pari, ever so caring, immediately believed me and insisted I rest. I felt a small pang of guilt for lying to her, but I knew this little deception was for her happiness.

Later that night, as my teammates and I settled into the train, Pari called again to check on me. My heart skipped a beat seeing her name flash on my phone. However, the noise inside the train was loud, with the constant chattering and the rumbling of wheels on the tracks. I panicked for a moment, worried that the background noise would give away my plan. Without thinking twice, I rushed to the washroom for some quiet.

"Hello?" I answered, trying to keep my voice steady.

"How are you feeling now?" she asked, her voice laced with concern.

"Better, much better," I replied, keeping my responses short, pretending to still be drowsy. Pari didn't want to disturb me too much, knowing I needed rest, so she didn't stay on the call for long. It was a brief exchange, but enough to feel her care even from miles away.

The next morning, as I stood in my hotel room with my teammates, Pari called again. "How are you feeling now?" she asked, her voice soft but persistent.

"I'm fine now, much better than last night," I replied. "But I think I'll take it easy today, just rest a bit more."

"Alright, take care, okay? Call me later in the afternoon if you feel better," she said.

"I will. I'll miss you, though," I replied, smiling to myself, knowing how close I was surprising her.

I had already planned everything in my head. I knew Pari would head to her college canteen for lunch. There was a beautiful fountain near the canteen, and I decided that would be the perfect spot to surprise her. I imagined her reaction, her wide eyes, and that radiant smile that I had missed so much. Just thinking about it made me more eager for the moment.

As I got ready, my heart raced with anticipation. The thought of seeing her again, after all this time, made every second feel like an eternity. I was ready to make her day unforgettable.

As I stood in the competition area, explaining our tech project to judges and curious onlookers, my mind was far from the presentation. All I could think about was Pari, when I'd finally get to see her and how she'd react to the surprise. Time felt like it was crawling, and I kept glancing at the clock, waiting for the afternoon to arrive.

In the midst of this, my phone buzzed. It was Pari checking on me. I knew she was on her way to the canteen with her friends, and this was the perfect chance to put my plan into motion. However, just as I tried to step away, a crowd started forming around our table, eager to see the project we were presenting. Feeling torn, I quickly handed over the presentation to one of my teammates and whispered, "Cover for me, please." Without waiting for a reply, I bolted toward the fountain where I knew Pari would pass by.

As I reached the fountain, slightly out of breath, I called her back. "Hey, how are you?" Pari asked as she picked up the call.

"I'm fine, ma," I replied, trying to keep my excitement from showing.

"Go and have a good lunch, okay? You'll feel better," Pari said in her caring tone.

Smiling to myself, I replied, "I know for sure I'm going to have a great lunch today."

She laughed lightly. "What? Why are you saying it like that? Are you high on medicine or something?" she teased.

I grinned and asked, "Where are you now?"

"I'm in college," she replied, sounding a bit confused.

"No, I mean, exactly where in college?" I asked again.

"I'm near the fountain, heading to the canteen," she replied casually. I looked around and spotted her immediately wearing a brown top and blue jeans, talking on the phone, completely unaware of my presence. My heart skipped a beat seeing her after so long.

"Oh, okay," I said, trying to hide the excitement in my voice.

"Why are you asking me so weirdly?" she asked, now suspicious.

"No reason, just curious," I replied, hiding behind a nearby pillar.

Then, a mischievous idea popped into my head. "Hey, Pari, you know Spider-Man, right?" I asked.

"Yeah, of course," she replied, amused by the sudden question.

"You know how he has that tingling Spidey sense?" I continued.

"Yes, I know," she replied, still walking casually, unknowingly passing right in front of me.

"Well, I think I have something like that too," I said.

"So, now you're Spider-Man?" Pari asked playfully, her voice filled with humour.

"No," I replied, grinning to myself, "I'm *your* man, ma. I have a sensation for you."

"Oh, really?" she replied, laughing. "What kind of sensation?"

"Turn around and see," I said, barely able to contain my excitement. "I'm getting goosebumps."

"What? What are you talking about?" she asked, confused.

"Just turn, ma," I said, stepping out from behind the pillar, standing near the fountain.

She turned, and as soon as her eyes landed on me, I saw her face light up in pure joy. For a moment, she froze, as if trying to process what was happening. Then, she jumped in excitement, her happiness so contagious it made my heart swell. She started to run toward me, but halfway through, she seemed to remember where she was—college, surrounded by her friends and classmates. She stopped herself from hugging me but came closer, her face filled with disbelief and happiness.

"What... what... are you doing here?" she stammered, her words barely forming as she tried to take in the surprise.

I smiled, trying to look as nonchalant as possible, but inside, I was just as thrilled as she was. "Surprise," I said softly.

She shook her head, still smiling, her eyes sparkling with joy. "You're unbelievable!" she finally managed to say, her voice trembling with emotion.

At that moment, the entire world seemed to fade away. It was just me and her, standing there, as if time had paused to let us soak in the happiness of seeing each other again.

I looked into her sparkling eyes, my heart racing as I asked, "So, how's the surprise, ma?"

She blinked, her cheeks flushing as she laughed lightly. "I think I'm Spider-Woman," she said humorously, her voice filled with warmth. "I had a tingling sense something big was going to happen when I got to see you."

We both burst into laughter, and for a moment, it felt like all the time and distance between us had melted away. I couldn't stop smiling, watching her grin so brightly. "You always know how to make me laugh, don't you?" I said, shaking my head playfully.

Then I looked at her and asked, "So, lunch with me? Just us?"

She paused, her face lighting up even more. "Of course," she replied, nodding eagerly.

At that moment, I remembered I had left my teammates back at the competition table. Feeling a slight pang of guilt, I quickly called them. "Hey, guys," I said on the phone. "I need to step out for a bit. I'll be back by 3, right before the final presentations."

My teammate laughed on the other end. "We figured you'd disappear after that reaction this morning. Go, enjoy. Just don't forget to be back in time!"

I smiled, grateful for their understanding, and hung up. Turning back to Pari, I said, "Alright, let's go. I know a great place around here."

She looked at me, her face glowing with happiness. "Lead the way," she said, and just like that, we started walking together, side by side.

Every step felt surreal. It wasn't just about seeing her; it was about the energy she brought with her, the way everything seemed brighter when she was around. And as we walked, laughing and catching up, I realized once again how much I cherished moments like these. Moments where nothing else mattered except us.

As we stepped out of the college gates, I hailed an auto and helped Pari get in, her excitement bubbling over. I had already picked out the perfect place, a cozy little restaurant I'd read about that was known for serving the best food in town. The ride was filled with her curious questions and my playful dodging of them, adding to the thrill of the moment.

When we arrived, the aroma of spices and freshly cooked meals welcomed us warmly. We found a corner table, away from the noise, where we could just talk and enjoy the moment. The food was delicious, but it wasn't just the meal that made it memorable, it was the company.

Throughout lunch, we talked about everything, especially how I had managed to pull off the whole surprise without her suspecting a thing.

"Ohhh, so that's why you were so happy that day when I called you and asked why!" Pari said, narrowing her eyes playfully. "And you said you were 'casual.'"

"Yep," I replied with a mischievous grin. "That was the moment I found out the news that the competition was at your college. I couldn't contain my happiness! I almost spilled everything, but then I thought, surprising you would be even better."

She shook her head, laughing. "You're unbelievable. I was so confused that day! I kept thinking, 'Why is he acting so weird?' But now it all makes sense. You really are full of surprises, aren't you?"

"Only for you, ma," I said, smiling. "Seeing your reaction today made it all worth it. The planning, the lies everything."

She laughed again, her eyes sparkling like they always did when she was truly happy. "It really was the best surprise," she said softly, her voice filled with emotion.

We spent the rest of lunch recounting every detail of my little scheme, how I avoided her calls, pretended to be sick, and even ran to the train's washroom to avoid suspicion. She couldn't stop giggling at my antics, and I couldn't stop watching her as she talked, her expressions animated, her laughter so genuine.

It was one of those moments I wanted to freeze in time, to keep replaying whenever life felt too overwhelming. Because nothing else mattered when we were together, sharing stories, laughing, and simply enjoying each other's presence.

We got back to the college around 2:30 PM, and I told Pari, "I'll finish the competition soon and meet you by 4 PM." She smiled and nodded, still buzzing from the surprise.

I went back to the competition hall, focused on my final presentation. As much as I enjoyed the experience, my mind kept wandering back to Pari. By 4 PM, I was done with everything and immediately rushed to meet her.

Our train was scheduled for 11 PM that night, so I told my teammates to head back to their hotel to rest, and assured them I'd meet them directly at the railway station. With that, I set off with Pari for what felt like the perfect ending to this day.

When we arrived at her house, her parents were surprised and happy to see me. I told them about the competition and how it had brought me to their city. They welcomed me warmly, and her dad even teased, "You're here for more than just the competition, aren't you?" I smiled, slightly embarrassed but happy to see they were so welcoming.

Pari, on the other hand, was bursting with excitement to show me around the house again. This time, it was fully furnished and complete, unlike the last time I'd visited. "See this? And this? We added this piece here after the housewarming," she said, pointing out every detail with pride.

I felt a pang of guilt for missing the housewarming function, but being here now, seeing her so happy, made up for it. As I walked through the rooms with her, it felt less like I was visiting her house and more like I was part of her world.

Dinner was served, and it felt like home. Her mom made all my favourite dishes, and we all sat together, talking and laughing. The warmth of her family reminded me of my own home, and I realized how lucky I was to have people who cared for me so deeply.

But as the clock struck 10 PM, it was finally time to go. My heart felt heavy, knowing I'd be leaving her again, but I didn't let it show. I hugged her parents goodbye and thanked them for their hospitality.

As Pari walked me to the gate, she was unusually quiet. "What's wrong, ma?" I asked softly.

"Nothing," she replied, forcing a smile. "It's just...it always feels so short when you're here."

I nodded, understanding exactly what she meant. "We'll have more time soon, ma. This is just the beginning."

She smiled faintly, and as I waved goodbye, I carried the memory of her sparkling eyes and that warm, glowing house in my heart.

As I called for an auto and got in to head to the railway station, I couldn't help but glance back. Pari stood there at the gate, her phone in hand, looking down at the screen. She hadn't moved, and I could feel her eyes, though distant, still following me.

Just as the auto started moving, my phone buzzed. A message popped up: *Happy journey, Partha.*

I smiled, a bittersweet smile that was a mix of joy and longing. I turned back from my seat in the auto and waved at her one last time. She looked up, noticed the wave, and smiled back. That small moment etched itself deep into my heart, as if the whole world had paused just for the two of us.

The journey to the railway station was quiet, yet my mind wasn't still. I replayed the surprise, her expressions, her laughter, and the way her face lit up when she saw me. Those memories made me smile all over again, but a part of me couldn't shake the sadness of leaving her behind.

When I got to the station, I reunited with my teammates, but my thoughts were still with Pari. Even on the train ride back to college, I felt the strange blend of happiness and emptiness. Happy because I had managed to surprise her and see her again, even if just for a day. Sad because I had left her behind once more, knowing it would be weeks before we could meet again.

Yet, as I sat in the moving train, I realized something. Even though we were miles apart, Pari had this way of making me feel close to her. Whether it was through her thoughtful messages, her care for my well-being, or just her presence in my memories, she had the power to make any distance feel like nothing.

That thought comforted me as I leaned back and stared out of the window at the passing lights, knowing I'd carry a piece of her with me wherever I went.

Then, my normal college routine started again, and everything fell back into place. It felt like life was on a roll, too good to be true, almost like a dream. Despite the distance between us, it didn't seem to matter in our relationship. Pari and I were managing it so well that it often surprised even me.

We stayed connected every day, no matter how busy things got on either end. The calls, the messages, the late-night conversations—they all became our lifeline. It felt like we were always a part of each other's lives, even though we were in different cities.

Of course, we weren't perfect. We did have our share of small fights, like any couple. But they were never big enough to leave any scars. They were the kind of silly fights where I'd tease her too much, or she'd get upset about me forgetting to call her back after class. Sometimes, it would be about me not taking care of myself, or her prioritizing studies over taking time to rest.

But one thing that always stood out was how we handled them. No matter how upset or annoyed we were, we never let a fight stretch into the night. We had an unspoken rule: no sleeping on a fight. By the time an hour or two passed, we'd always sort it out. A heartfelt apology, a funny meme, or a cute voice message—one of us would break the ice, and it would be back to normal.

It felt reassuring. No matter how much life threw at us, Pari and I always found a way to come back to each other. It wasn't just about love; it was about understanding, compromise, and genuinely wanting to make things work.

And in those moments, I realized how lucky I was. Even though we weren't physically together, I never felt alone. Pari had this way of making me feel cared for, even from miles away. And that, more than anything, made me believe that no matter how far apart we were, we'd always find our way back to each other.

Then, my normal college routine started again, and everything fell back into place. It felt like life was on a roll, too good to be true, almost like a dream. Despite the distance between us, it didn't seem to matter in our relationship. Pari and I were managing it so well that it often surprised even me.

We stayed connected every day, no matter how busy things got on either end. The calls, the messages, the late-night conversations—they all became our lifeline. It felt like we were always a part of each other's lives, even though we were in different cities.

Of course, we weren't perfect. We did have our share of small fights, like any couple. But they were never big enough to leave any scars. They were the kind of silly fights where I'd tease her too much, or she'd get upset about me forgetting to call her back after class. Sometimes, it would be about me not taking care of myself, or her prioritizing studies over taking time to rest.

But one thing that always stood out was how we handled them. No matter how upset or annoyed we were, we never let a fight stretch into the night. We had an unspoken rule: no sleeping on a fight. By the time an hour or two passed, we'd always sort it out. A heartfelt apology, a funny meme, or a cute voice message—one of us would break the ice, and it would be back to normal.

It felt reassuring. No matter how much life threw at us, Pari and I always found a way to come back to each other. It wasn't just about love; it was about understanding, compromise, and genuinely wanting to make things work.

And in those moments, I realized how lucky I was. Even though we weren't physically together, I never felt alone. Pari had this way of making me feel cared for, even from miles away. And that, more than anything, made me believe that no matter how far apart we were, we'd always find our way back to each other.

The days were going by smoothly, and my birthday was approaching. Last year, because of the lockdown and restrictions, we didn't get the chance to celebrate our birthdays together. To be honest, I was never really fond of my birthday.

It wasn't because I didn't like celebrations—it was because my birthday reminded me of the day I first found out that Pari was leaving town. That was the day I realized my feelings for her, and ever since, my birthday always carried a bittersweet memory with it. So, even this time, I wasn't particularly excited about it.

But Pari had different plans.

The day before my birthday, she suddenly went silent. She didn't respond to any of my messages or calls, which was very unlike her. At first, I thought she was busy with college or maybe had fallen asleep early. But as the hours passed, the silence started bothering me. I kept checking my phone, waiting for a reply, but there was nothing.

Even at night, when we always talked before sleeping, there was no call from her. It felt strange. A part of me was worried—was she upset with me? Did I say something wrong? Or was something bothering her? I wanted to call again, but I didn't want to seem too clingy, so I decided to wait

I waited for a long time, but as the minutes passed, my patience wore thin. I couldn't take it anymore—I called her again at 11 PM, but still, there was no answer. My heart started pounding with worry. I sent her multiple messages, hoping for even a single reply, but nothing came. Fear started creeping into my mind. Had something happened? Was she okay?

As the clock neared 11:45 PM, I was too anxious to sit still. I decided to step onto the terrace to get some fresh air and clear my head while waiting for her response. But the moment I reached there, I froze.

There she was—Pari—standing with my friends, holding a cake, smiling and talking to them. They were all waiting for the clock to strike exactly midnight to surprise me. A wave of emotions hit me all at once. Relief, happiness, and guilt for overthinking everything.

For a second, I just stood there, overwhelmed. I wanted to run down and hug her tightly, to tell her how worried I had been and how much I had missed her all day. But at the same time, I didn't want to ruin her surprise.

So, taking a deep breath and suppressing my excitement, I quietly made my way back to my flat. I sat on the sofa, pretending to be lost in my phone, knowing that any minute now, the door would open, and Pari would walk in, making this night truly unforgettable.

Then, at exactly 11:59 PM, there was a knock on the door. I already knew who it was—my friends and Pari. But I had to keep up the act, so I put on my best "confused" face, got up, and opened the door.

There stood my friends, grinning. And hiding behind them, peeking out like a little kid playing hide-and-seek, was Pari. I looked at them, pretending to be clueless, and the next second, Pari jumped out from behind, yelling, **"Surprise! Happy birthday!"**

Her smile was so wide, I swear her cheeks must have been hurting. She was *that* happy. Seeing her like that, my heart melted. I played along, acting all surprised before pulling her into a hug.

I invited everyone in, and that's when I noticed something—Pari had never met my college friends before, yet somehow, she had managed to find them all and plan this. That made me even more emotional. But at the same time, I felt a little awkward. Despite being friends with these guys for months, I had never told them about my relationship with Pari. They only knew her as my "best friend."

Now, though? There was no hiding it. The way she looked at me, the way she had planned everything—it was obvious. My friends gave me those *side-eyes* as they walked in, smirking at me, as if saying, **"Best friend, huh?"**

We cut the cake, had a small but heartwarming celebration, and spent the night laughing and making memories. One by one, my friends left, heading back to their places. But Pari? She stayed back.

She had planned an entire day with me tomorrow, and honestly? That was the best gift I could ever ask for.

As all of my friends left and only Pari remained, she suddenly hugged me tightly from behind. Her warmth, her presence—it felt like home.

*"How was the surprise, Partha?"* she asked softly, her voice filled with excitement.

I smiled, still taking in everything that had just happened. *"It was beautiful, maa. I really felt special,"* I replied honestly. But then, I sighed and added, *"I was worried, though. You didn't pick up my calls the whole day. I was really tense."*

Pari chuckled and turned me around to face her. *"That was all part of the plan, Partha. By making you tense first and then surprising you, I made sure the moment was even more special. You're not the only one who knows how to pull off a surprise visit—I can too!"* she said with a playful grin.

I couldn't help but smile to myself. *"I knew it... 15 minutes before,"* I murmured, recalling how I had spotted her on the terrace. But I didn't tell her that—I let her enjoy her victory.

Then, looking into her eyes, I said, *"Come on, let's go out for a short ride around the city."*

It was late, but I didn't care. I just wanted to spend more time with her. Just the two of us, under the stars, making this night even more unforgettable.

Then we hopped onto my scooty and took off, riding through the quiet streets of the city. I showed her all the places that had become a part of my daily life—my college, the restaurants where I had lunch, the little spots I often visited. I wanted her to see everything, to be part of this world I had built here.

After a while, we stumbled upon a cozy café that was still open late at night. We decided to stop there for a cup of coffee, just sitting across from each other, soaking in the moment. The warmth of the coffee, the silence of the night, and the presence of Pari made everything feel surreal.

By the time we got back to my house, it was already around 2 AM. Pari had everything planned for the next day from 9AM in the morning, so I knew I had to wake up at least by 8 AM. We decided to call it a night.

I went to grab a blanket for her when she looked at me and asked, *"Why?"*

*"I'll sleep on the couch. You can take my bed,"* I replied.

And then she burst out laughing—so hard that she nearly fell off the bed.

*"What?"* I asked, confused.

*"You come here, idiot,"* Pari said, grabbing my hand and pulling me toward her. *"Come sleep with me. You don't have to*

*sleep on the couch, you fool."*

Before I could protest, she playfully pushed me onto the bed and snuggled close, lying on my chest.

Suddenly, I felt butterflies in my stomach, and my heart started racing uncontrollably. I knew she could feel it too.

Pari giggled and teased, *"My head is bouncing because of your heartbeat!"*

I smiled, feeling both nervous and at peace. She wrapped her arms around me tightly—so tight that I could barely breathe properly. But in that moment, I didn't care. It was too beautiful, too perfect to ruin with words.

Then she looked up at me with those deep, sparkling eyes and whispered, *"Partha, do you know how many times I've dreamt of sleeping on your chest and holding you so tightly? It was the one thing I wanted the most—to fall asleep in your arms every night."*

Hearing those words, my heart swelled with emotions. I gently kissed her forehead and whispered back, *"Now you can."*

She chuckled softly, her grip around me tightening even more. I smiled and whispered into her ear, *"Good night, Pari maa."*

With a sleepy voice, she whispered back, *"Good night, Partha,"* before drifting off into sleep, her breath warm against my chest.

She was exhausted from all the traveling, and soon, she was fast asleep, lying on me like a little child—peaceful, serene, and beautiful. I, on the other hand, couldn't sleep. I was too mesmerized by the way she looked, the way she breathed so softly, the way she adjusted herself against me, rubbing her head gently against my chest to find the perfect spot.

I ran my fingers through her soft hair, caressing her head, and gently patted her back, making sure she slept comfortably. She let out a little sigh, as if telling me she was at peace.

And gradually, with her warmth against me, her heartbeat syncing with mine, I, too, drifted off into sleep—holding onto the most beautiful moment of my life

I had one of the most peaceful sleeps in a long time. When I woke up in the morning, the bed beside me was empty. I stretched and got up, wondering where Pari had gone.

As I stepped out of the room, a familiar, comforting aroma filled the air—coffee. I smiled to myself. Pari was already awake and making coffee for me.

I walked up behind her, planning to scare her, but before I could even try, she turned around and caught me.

*"Good morning, Pari,"* I said, leaning against the counter.

*"Oh, you're up already? I wanted to wake you up with a coffee,"* she said, handing me a cup.

*"It's okay, I'll have it now,"* I replied, taking the warm cup from her hands.

We both walked to the balcony, letting the morning breeze hit our faces as we sipped on our coffee. I looked at her and said, *"It's been so long since somebody made me coffee in the morning. Every day, I've been making it for myself."*

She smiled at me and nudged my arm playfully. *"Well, now you have me. But don't get used to it!"* she joked.

I chuckled, taking another sip.

*"Now drink your coffee fast and get ready. We have to go to the temple,"* she said, her excitement evident in her voice.

After finishing our coffee, I got up to freshen up, and Pari did the same.

Our first stop for the day was the temple. As soon as we arrived, the peaceful atmosphere filled me with a sense of calm. After offering our prayers, Pari gently placed a small pinch of kumkum on my forehead. At that moment, I felt something indescribable—warmth, love, and a deep sense of belonging.

After the temple visit, Pari insisted we go for breakfast. I wasn't really hungry, but she wouldn't take no for an answer. *"You have to eat something,"* she said firmly. So, we went to a small eatery nearby and had a simple yet fulfilling breakfast.

The rest of the day was spent roaming around the city, exploring different places, talking endlessly, and making the most of our time together. As the evening approached, we found ourselves strolling through a busy street lined with vendors selling various trinkets.

That's when my eyes fell on a small stall selling beaded bracelets. There was something about them—so simple, yet something about them caught my attention. Pari noticed me staring at them and, without a second thought, pulled me towards the stall.

*"You like it, don't you?"* she asked, smiling.

Before I could even reply, she picked up one and placed it on my wrist. *"This one suits you,"* she said and bought it for me.

It was just ₹30, something small and ordinary. But when Pari gave it to me, it became priceless.

I thanked Pari for the bracelet, feeling grateful for such a thoughtful gesture. As we continued walking through the street, my eyes landed on a jewellery store with a display of silver bracelets. One, in particular, caught my attention—it had a delicate butterfly charm.

I immediately thought of Pari. She adored butterflies. Every time we talked on the phone while she was out for her evening walks, she would mention how butterflies fluttered around her, almost as if they followed her. It was something that always made her happy.

Without wasting a moment, I turned to her and said, *"Pari, can you get me a bottle of water?"* She nodded and walked towards a nearby stall while I rushed into the jewellery store.

As I stood at the billing counter, my phone rang—it was Pari.

*"Where are you, Partha?"* she asked curiously.

I quickly came up with an excuse. *"Uh... I'm in the restroom. Just wait there, I'll be back soon."*

I paid for the bracelet in a hurry. There wasn't enough time to get it wrapped, so I just slipped it into my jacket pocket and rushed back to meet her.

*"What took you so long?"* Pari asked the moment I returned.

*"The restroom was crowded,"* I lied smoothly, hoping she wouldn't get suspicious.

After wandering around for a little longer, we decided to head back to the apartment. Pari had her train scheduled for 12:45 AM, and as much as I wanted time to slow down, I knew our beautiful day was coming to an end.

It was around 7:30 PM when we returned to my apartment. I told Pari that I would cook dinner for her as part of my birthday celebration. She insisted on helping, so she chopped some vegetables while I prepared biryani and chicken masala.

When we finally sat down to eat, the food turned out to be incredibly delicious. They say the secret ingredient to good food is love—but since we both cooked it together, it had *double* the love, making it taste even better. We laughed about it as we ate, cherishing every moment.

Time flew by, and soon it was 10:30 PM. As I was cleaning up, Pari suddenly hugged me from behind. At first, I was surprised, but then I heard a soft sob.

*"Pari, what happened, maa?"* I asked gently.

She sniffled and whispered, *"I don't want to leave, Partha. I want it to stay just like this... the way it's been since last night. I want to be with you every minute."*

Hearing her say that broke my heart a little. I turned around to face her, wiping away the tear that escaped her eye. I wished I could freeze time, hold her close, and never let her go.

*"It will happen, maa, but it will take some time—that's all. Now don't cry, it's a happy birthday, right? Not a sad birthday. Let's make it cheerful, maa! We'll talk again tomorrow on a video call and everything."*

I gently wiped away her tears, trying to bring back that beautiful smile of hers.

Pari sniffled and nodded, her lips curving into a small smile. I always knew how to cheer her up, just like she knew how to do the same for me. No matter how sad either of us felt, we always found a way to lift each other up. That was the kind of bond we had—strong, unbreakable, and filled with love.

Afterwards, Pari started packing, and we left the apartment around 11:45 PM to head to the railway station a bit early. I carried her bag into the train, found her seat, and then sat on a bench on the platform. We were both trying hard not to cry as we prepared to part ways again.

As the time approached, we heard the announcement that the train was about to depart. Pari stepped into the train and stood at the door. We looked into each other's eyes, and just as the train honked, I suddenly remembered the bracelet I had bought for her. I quickly took it out and handed it to her.

"I know how much you love butterflies," I said. "This is a small return gift for everything you did for me today. This was the best birthday of my life, and I would never forget it, even if I got more lives. You are my butterfly—you're as majestic and beautiful as one. I may not love butterflies as much as you do, but I love you more than you love them."

I could see tears welling up in her eyes. She looked at me and asked, "Why are you giving this to me now? We were together the whole day. Why not earlier?"

I chuckled. "Then it wouldn't have been as filmy and romantic as it is now."

She smiled through her tears. "You're such an idiot and a filmy romantic, Parth."

The train started moving. I looked at her and grinned. "Now we can even recreate SRK's *Dilwale Dulhania Le Jayenge* scene. Just a little different—this time, instead of Raj pulling Simran, Simran would have to pull Raj. What do you say?"

She chuckled and, with a teary-eyed smile, said, "I love you so much, Partha."

I smiled and replied, "I love you too."

Even though we were parting again, we were happy. It was a perfect day and a beautiful farewell for the night.

# 6

# Shattered Thread...

The days were going so well, and the whole year passed by in a blur. We met once every two months, and sometimes even twice in a month. Despite the distance, we never let it feel like a barrier between us. We were genuinely happy, cherishing every moment we got together.

But happiness never stays untouched forever. No matter how perfect things seem, there's always a small crack waiting to appear. And in our story, that crack came in the form of a slight misunderstanding.

A tiny misunderstanding,something so small that we didn't even think it mattered. But it did. It mattered a lot.

Like a drop of lemon juice that can spoil liters of milk, that one misunderstanding slowly started to change everything between us.

I was happily listening to Pari talk about her friends, laughing at their stories, and enjoying the way she spoke so fondly of them. I was okay with all of her friends,well, almost all.

There was one guy I wasn't too sure about. Something about the way she described his actions, the way he always seemed to be around, made me feel uneasy. I didn't say anything at first, thinking maybe I was overreacting. But as she continued talking, I started piecing things together. His gestures, his timing, the way he always seemed to be there for her,it wasn't just friendship.

I could sense it in his actions, even though Pari, in her innocence, didn't see it. She had no idea what was really happening.

I didn't want to be that jealous boyfriend who tells his girl who she can or can't be friends with. Pari truly saw him as a friend, and I respected that. But I didn't think he felt the same way about her.

For a whole month, I listened to her stories about him,how he helped her, how he was always there, how he did little things that she found sweet but that I knew had a different meaning. I kept my feelings to myself, not wanting to create an issue where there might not be one.

But no matter how much I tried to ignore it, the uneasy feeling inside me wouldn't go away. It started bothering me more and more. I realized I couldn't keep hiding my thoughts from Pari. She needed to know what I was seeing, what I was feeling.

So, I decided,it was time to tell her.

I gently asked Pari to clear things up with him, to make sure that they were truly just friends and that there were no hidden feelings on his side.

"Why?" she asked, confused.

"I don't think he's doing all of this just for friendship," I said honestly.

Pari sighed. "I know him, Partha. He doesn't have any intentions like that."

"Just make it clear, ma," I insisted.

She looked at me, her eyes searching mine. "Don't you trust me?" she asked softly.

I took a deep breath. "I trust you so much, ma. I know you. But I don't trust a random stranger."

"He's not a stranger. He's my friend," she replied firmly.

"But for me, he is a stranger," I said.

Pari frowned. "I don't see your friends as strangers. I see them as friends."

"I do too, ma," I said. "But not about this one."

And just like that, what started as a simple conversation turned into a stretched-out debate. The more we talked, the more stubborn we became. Slowly, our discussion turned into a heated argument, one neither of us saw coming.

Pari hung up the video call. It was the first time we had ever fought over a video call. Usually, whenever we argued, just looking into each other's eyes would be enough to let go of everything. But this time was different.

That day, she didn't call me. For the past two years, we had an unspoken rule,no matter how small or big the fight was, we would always clear things up before going to sleep. But that night, she didn't call.

And I didn't call either.

Because I was angry too.

The next morning, I thought about what had happened the night before. Maybe I had been too overprotective, trying to keep her away from her friends. Love has that kind of jealousy,it makes you want to keep your favorite person only for yourself. I can't say it's bad, but it's not entirely good either. It's just a natural human tendency.

Realizing this, I decided to call her in the morning. By that time, she had already left for college. But she didn't pick up my call.

Then, in the evening, I finally got a call from Pari.

"Hello," she said in a low voice.

Hearing her like that broke my heart. Guilt started creeping in,I hadn't meant to make her this sad. Yes, I was angry last night, but I never wanted to hurt her like this.

"I'm sorry, Pari," I said immediately. "I was too angry, ma. I acted immaturely. I'm really sorry."

"It's okay, Partha," she said softly.

But I could still hear the sadness in her voice. It wasn't okay.

"I will do anything to make you happy, ma. Tell me what I can do," I pleaded.

"You can't do anything, Partha," she said.

"I'm sorry," I repeated.

"It's okay. I know long distance is hard, and feeling jealous is normal," she said.

"But I'm still sorry," I insisted.

"I'm sorry too," she admitted. "I argued too. I should have just said yes."

Then we both compromised and got into a slightly better mood, but that incident left a small crack in our relationship, a black dot that neither of us acknowledged out loud but both silently carried with us. It wasn't like before, where every little misunderstanding would be resolved with a laugh or a heartfelt apology. This time, there was something different,a shift in the air between us, a lingering hesitation in our conversations.

Pari, being the caring person she was, gradually stopped mentioning that guy altogether. At first, I didn't even notice it. But as days passed, I realized that the stories she used to tell me so excitedly,the little moments about her college life, the silly things her friends did,were missing a part. She had started filtering what she told me, carefully choosing her words, ensuring she never brought up that guy again. Maybe she was doing it to avoid another argument, maybe just to make me feel secure, or maybe, deep down, she feared that another misunderstanding could widen the crack that had already formed between us.

I should have felt reassured, knowing that she was being considerate of my feelings. But instead, it made me uneasy. It felt like we were both pretending, like we were walking on eggshells around something that had already left a scar. I wanted to tell her that she didn't have to do that, that I trusted her, that she could talk to me about anything. But every time I thought of bringing it up, a strange fear stopped me,what if bringing it up made things worse? What if, instead of fixing it, we ended up reopening a wound that was still healing?

So, I let it be. We moved forward, or at least, we tried to. We laughed, we loved, we talked for hours like we always did. But in the quiet moments, when the conversation slowed and the laughter faded, I couldn't help but wonder,had we really moved on, or were we just pretending everything was fine?

And after a month or so had passed, I found myself drowning in stress. College assignments were piling up, deadlines were looming over me like dark clouds, and the extracurricular activities I had committed to started to feel overwhelming. My entire schedule had become so hectic that I barely had a moment to breathe. The pressure kept building, and I noticed that my temper was becoming short. I would get frustrated over the smallest things, my patience was thinning, and I felt like I was carrying an unbearable weight on my shoulders.

In times like these, there was only one person who could instantly bring me peace,Pari. Just hearing her voice had the power to calm the storm inside me. It had been a long day, and I hadn't even spoken to her properly in the last couple of days because of how busy I was. I realized that I needed her. I needed to talk to her, to listen to her voice, to feel the warmth in her words. Maybe, just maybe, she could pull me out of this irritated and exhausted state.

So, without thinking twice, I picked up my phone and dialed her number. As the call started ringing, I leaned back on my chair, closing my eyes, hoping that as soon as she answered, her voice would wash away all my stress.

As she answered the call, I could hear a lot of noise in the background,people talking, cups clinking, the general hum of a busy place.

"I'm in a café, Partha. I'll call you later," she said quickly and hung up before I could even respond.

I stared at my phone for a few seconds, feeling a little cranky about it. I had been looking forward to hearing her voice, hoping she would bring me some peace, but instead, the call lasted barely five seconds. Still, I didn't react. I told myself she must be busy and that she would call me back when she was free.

That day, I had to stay late at college, caught up in some extra work. By the time I finally left, it was already past 8 PM. The whole day had drained every ounce of energy from me, and all I wanted to do was go home and sleep.

As soon as I reached my apartment, I threw my bag on the floor, kicked off my shoes, and collapsed onto the couch, not even bothering to change my clothes. Within minutes, exhaustion took over, and I fell into a deep sleep.

Then, at around 9:30 PM, I was jolted awake by the vibration of my phone. My eyes were still heavy with sleep, and I groggily reached for it.

It was Pari.

I picked up the call.

"Hello," said Pari.

"Hello," I replied, my voice still groggy from sleep.

"Are you fine?" she asked, sounding a bit concerned.

"Yeah, I'm fine," I replied, rubbing my eyes.

"But you don't sound well," she insisted.

"I was asleep," I admitted.

"Oh, okay then. I'll call you tomorrow," Pari said.

"No, it's okay. Talk to me. I still have to change my clothes anyway," I replied, sitting up and stretching.

She started talking, telling me about her day,how her classes went, something funny her professor said, a random thing she saw on the way home. I listened, nodding along, but something felt off. I realized she hadn't mentioned the café at all, even though that was where she had been when she cut my call earlier.

So I asked, "What about the café?"

"It was fine," she replied casually.

"Fine? You spent hours there, and it's just fine?" I asked, trying to make sense of her answer.

"Yep," she replied quickly.

That's when I caught on. Something was off. Pari wasn't talking the way she usually did. Her tone had changed slightly, and it felt like she was deliberately steering the conversation away from the café topic. She was always so detailed about the smallest things, but now she was brushing it off like it didn't matter.

I leaned back on the couch, suddenly more awake. Something about this didn't feel right.

"Is everything alright, Pari?" I asked, my voice softer now, trying to understand what was going on.

"Yes," she replied, but I could hear something in her voice,something hesitant, something that didn't quite match the usual way she spoke to me.

"Then why are you acting weird?" I pressed.

There was a pause. Then she finally said, with a bit of guilt in her voice, "I didn't go to the café with all my friends."

And that was it. That one sentence made everything click in my mind. I suddenly knew why she hadn't talked about the café, why she had avoided the topic altogether. She was trying to keep that guy out of the conversation. She just wanted to make me feel secure.

I knew it. I understood why she did it. But in that moment, it didn't feel okay. It felt like something had cracked between us.

"Bye, Pari," I said abruptly.

"Partha, he is just a friend. It was just a friends' outing," she tried to explain.

But I had already lost my temper. The stress from college, the pressure I had been feeling for weeks, the exhaustion,it all mixed with this moment. I couldn't control my emotions anymore. Without thinking, I just hung up the call.

After hanging up the call, my frustration only grew stronger. I felt like a pressure cooker about to explode. In that moment of rage, I grabbed the glass lying on the table and threw it across the room. It shattered into tiny pieces, the sound echoing through the silence of my apartment.

I took a deep breath, trying to calm myself down. I didn't want to think about it anymore. I had reports to complete, so I pulled out my laptop, hoping that drowning myself in work would help me escape the thoughts running wild in my head.

As I typed, my phone vibrated twice. Pari was calling. I saw her name flashing on the screen, but I couldn't bring myself to answer. I was still angry, still stubborn, still letting my ego take over. I ignored both calls.

A whole day passed before I finally gave in. I couldn't keep running away from this. So, I called her.

"Hello," she answered, her voice steady, but I could tell she was still upset. She wasn't her usual self.

I sighed. "I'm sorry, Pari," I said, my voice softer now. "I was rude. I was jealous. I shouldn't have acted like that."

There was a pause. Then she finally said, "It's okay, Partha."

But I could hear it in her tone, she had forgiven me, but something still lingered between us. The fight was no longer a raging fire, but it was like an ember covered in ash, still burning underneath.

Days went by, and we never really talked about our fight. We just let it fade into the background, pretending it didn't exist. But something had changed. Our conversations became a little less frequent, a little less vibrant. It wasn't like before, when we could talk for hours without running out of things to say. Now, there were pauses, gaps, moments of silence that neither of us knew how to fill.

Then, my birthday arrived.

I wasn't particularly excited this time. But last year, Pari had made it so special that, despite myself, I had started to expect something again. Four years ago, my birthday was just another day. Nothing extraordinary. But ever since Pari entered my life, birthdays had felt different. Special. And last year, she made it the best one yet.

This time, though, I already knew she wasn't coming to town. She had called me in the evening, and I could hear it in her voice, she was still at home, miles away.

It was 11:50 PM. I had my phone in my hand, waiting. Pari still hadn't texted me, called me, or sent any message.

I thought maybe she was planning a surprise video call at midnight, something special, like last year. So, I waited.

11:59 PM.

I was convinced she was just pretending to be offline, that she would suddenly pop up at 12 AM and surprise me.

Then, the clock struck 12.

I stared at my phone, waiting for it to ring. Any second now, Pari would call. Any second...

But nothing happened.

I told myself she might have gotten a little late. Maybe her internet was slow, or maybe she was setting up something sweet before calling. So I kept waiting.

12:05 AM. No call.

12:10 AM. Still nothing.

12:15 AM. Silence.

Not even a text.

It wasn't just Pari. No one else had called either,except for my parents. And that's when it hit me.

I had been so caught up in my own world, in my fights with Pari, in my endless workload, that I had been pushing everyone else away. My friends, the people who had always been there, were nowhere to be seen tonight. And maybe it wasn't their fault. Maybe I had been the one avoiding them all along.

Around 12:40 AM, one of my friends noticed it was my birthday through Snapchat and sent me a message. Slowly, more wishes started coming in,one after another. My phone started buzzing with notifications, yet none of them were from the one person I was waiting for.

I kept staring at my screen, hoping for just one message from Pari. But it never came.

As the minutes passed, my heart grew heavier. The excitement I had felt earlier turned into disappointment. The one person who made my birthday feel special last year... wasn't here this time.

Tears welled up in my eyes as I sat there, holding my phone, waiting, just waiting for her.

I didn't sleep the entire night. No matter how hard I tried to distract myself, my mind kept going back to that one missing wish.

Then, around 6 AM, exhausted and drained, I decided to take a bath. Maybe the cold water would wake me up, make me feel better.

As I stepped out, my eyes immediately went to my phone. And there it was, a long birthday message from Pari.

For a moment, it felt nice. Her words were sweet, thoughtful, and filled with love. But deep down, I couldn't shake off the feeling that something was missing.

If only she had sent it at midnight. If only she had called. If only...

As soon as I replied, "Thank you, Pari," my phone started ringing. It was her.

I picked up, and the first thing I heard was her crying.

"I'm so sorry, Partha," she sobbed. "I really wanted to call you at midnight and read all of this to you, but I got a headache... and I fell asleep."

I could hear the guilt in her voice, the way it broke between her cries.

"It's okay, ma," I said softly, trying to calm her down. "Thank you so much for wishing me. How's your headache now?"

"It's okay now... but leave that, Partha. I'm so, so sorry," she repeated.

I sighed. Even though my heart still carried a little sting from last night, hearing her like this made me push it aside.

"It's okay, ma," I reassured her again.

I didn't tell her that I had cried at night. I didn't want her to feel even more guilty about it.

That day, we both skipped our classes. Instead, we spent the whole day talking,about everything and nothing. It felt like old times, like we had somehow stepped back into the beginning, where there were no fights, no misunderstandings,just us.

For the first time in a while, things felt light again.

And from that day on, it started to feel like a relationship again. Like how it felt at first.

Then, one random evening, as I was walking through the park, I suddenly felt something off on my wrist,like something had just brushed against it. Instinctively, I looked down.

The red cord that Pari had tied to my wrist years ago had fallen off.

It lay there on the ground, motionless.

For three years, it had stayed intact, through everything,never once loosening, never once breaking. And now, all of a sudden, it had fallen.

A bad omen.

For a brief moment, an unsettling thought crossed my mind. But I quickly brushed it away. After all, it had gone through wear and tear for years. It was bound to snap at some point, right?

I bent down, picked it up, and slipped it into my pocket.

Then, without thinking much of it, I continued walking.

After two days, one night, Pari called.

"Partha, I want to talk to you about something."

"What, ma?" I asked.

"Please don't call me 'ma,'" Pari replied.

My heart shattered.

"What? Why?" I asked, my voice shaking.

There was silence on the other end for a moment before she spoke again.

"I think, Partha... we need to take a break. We're constantly fighting now, and this distance is making it even harder for us."

For a second, everything around me blurred. It felt like the ground beneath me had crumbled.

I felt my heart skip a beat. My hands turned cold, and I gripped the phone tighter as if holding onto it could somehow hold onto her.

"Pari... what are you saying?" I asked, my voice barely above a whisper.

There was a long pause. I could hear her breathing on the other end, shaky and uneven. It felt like she was struggling just as much as I was.

"You know exactly what I mean, Partha," she finally said. Her voice was soft but firm, carrying the weight of something she had been holding in for a long time.

"No, I don't," I insisted, my voice rising slightly. "I don't understand why you're suddenly saying this. Just a few days ago, everything felt normal. We talked, we laughed, we,"

"But we also fought," she cut me off. "Partha, don't you see? We're not the same anymore. The fights, the misunderstandings, the distance... it's all becoming too much."

I ran a hand through my hair, trying to steady myself. "Pari, every relationship has fights. It doesn't mean we give up. We always fix things, don't we?"

She sighed deeply. "I know, Partha. But lately, it feels like we're fixing things more than we're enjoying them. I don't want our relationship to turn into something that only survives on apologies and compromises."

Her words felt like a dagger to my chest. I opened my mouth to argue, to say something,anything,to change her mind. But for the first time, I didn't have the right words.

"Is this because of that guy?" I finally asked, my voice laced with frustration and desperation.

"Partha, stop," she pleaded. "It's not about him. It's about us. We've changed, and I don't know if we're making each other happy anymore."

I clenched my jaw, feeling my emotions spiral out of control. "So, what do you want, Pari? Do you want to leave me? Just like that?"

She sniffled, and I knew she was crying. "I don't want to leave you, Partha. That's the last thing I want. But I also don't want us to keep hurting each other like this."

"Then don't say things like this!" I almost shouted, my voice breaking. "We can fix this, Pari. Just like we always do."

There was another painful silence before she spoke again, her voice barely above a whisper.

"Maybe we need time apart... to understand what we really want."

I felt my heart shatter into a million pieces. I wanted to argue, to tell her she was wrong, that we didn't need space,we needed each other. But deep down, a part of me feared that maybe she was right. Maybe things really had changed.

"Pari... please," I whispered, my voice almost begging.

"I love you, Partha," she said, and I could hear her voice tremble. "And that's exactly why I think we need this."

Tears welled up in my eyes. "I love you too, Pari. But I don't know how to do this without you."

"You will," she said. "We both will."

And just like that, the call ended.

I stared at the phone screen, my mind refusing to accept what had just happened. My hands trembled, my chest felt heavy, and a hollow emptiness started spreading inside me.

Pari was my everything. And now, for the first time in years, I was standing at a crossroad without her.

Days passed, and I still couldn't wrap my head around what had happened. One moment, we were fine,at least, I thought we were,and the next, everything fell apart.

I kept rereading our old messages, searching for signs, for clues, for anything that could tell me where it went wrong. But I found nothing. Nothing that could justify why we had to be apart.

I called her,no answer.
I texted her,left on read.

It hurt more than anything. Pari, the one person who always replied, always cared, was now silent.

I knew she was hurting just as much as I was. But if she was hurting, why wasn't she talking to me? Why was she pushing me away?

I couldn't take it anymore. I sent her another message.

"Pari, please. Just talk to me. I don't understand what's happening. If we love each other, why are we doing this? Please, don't shut me out."

Hours passed. No reply.

I stared at my screen, my heart aching. I typed another message.

"I'm sorry, Pari. For everything. Just tell me what to do, and I'll do it. But don't walk away like this. Please."

Still nothing.

The silence was unbearable. It was like she had disappeared, like we had never existed. The memories of us,of our late-night talks, our laughter, our fights, our love,felt like they were slipping through my fingers, and I was powerless to stop it.

I didn't know what to do anymore. Should I keep trying? Should I wait? Should I let her go?

I lay on my bed, staring at the ceiling, my mind racing with a million thoughts. The red thread she had once tied around my wrist was still on my table, broken, just like us.

Then it hit me,love is so fragile. It wasn't about the big moments, the grand gestures, or the promises of forever. It was about the little things, the everyday moments, the patience, and the unspoken understanding between two hearts. And somehow, somewhere along the way, I had let all of that slip through my fingers.

If I had just been a little more understanding...
If I had just let go of my ego instead of letting it build walls between us...
If I had just trusted her a little more instead of letting my insecurities take over...

Maybe, just maybe, Pari would still be here.

The weight of that realization crushed me. It felt like someone had reached inside my chest and squeezed my heart until it ached. I kept replaying every moment, every fight, every misunderstanding,wondering what I could have done differently, how I could have saved us before it was too late.

I thought about the first time we met, the way her eyes lit up when she spoke about things she loved, the way she would call me maa just to tease me, the way she knew exactly how to make me smile even on my worst days. I thought about the late-night conversations, the way we laughed until our stomachs hurt, the quiet moments when we didn't have to say anything at all, yet everything felt right.

And now, silence.

A silence so loud, it drowned out everything else.

I stared at my phone, hoping, praying, begging for a message, a call, anything to tell me that this wasn't real, that she would come back. But there was nothing. My messages stayed on read. My calls went unanswered. And with each passing second, reality sank deeper into my soul,I had lost her.

I wanted to scream, to cry, to turn back time and fix everything, but life doesn't give second chances that easily. Love, no matter how deep, cannot survive without care. And I had let mine wither away, thinking it was invincible.

I thought about that red thread, the one she had tied on my wrist years ago, the one that had stayed with me for three years without breaking. And then, just two days before she said goodbye, it had fallen off.

Maybe it wasn't just wear and tear.

Maybe it was a sign.

Maybe our love, just like that thread, had worn out.

I reached into my pocket and pulled out the broken thread, running my fingers over it gently, as if I could somehow piece it back together,just like I wished I could do with us. But some things, once broken, can never be the same again.

A tear slipped down my cheek, followed by another, until I was sobbing, my entire body shaking with the weight of everything I had lost. I wasn't just crying for Pari. I was crying for us, for the love that could have been, for the future we had dreamed of but would never get to live.

And in that moment, I finally understood,

Love isn't just about finding the right person.

It's about holding on to them, even when it's hard.

It's about choosing them, every single day, despite the fights, despite the doubts, despite the distance.

But I had learned this lesson too late.

And now, all I had left was an empty heart, a broken thread, and the ghost of a love that once was.

# 7
## The Shadow of Her Light...

It was just another ordinary day. I was walking down a familiar street, lost in my own thoughts, when something caught my eye a little girl tugging at her father's sleeve, her voice filled with excitement and urgency.

"Please, Daddy! I need the unicorn keychain!" she pleaded, her tiny fingers pointing at the trinket hanging in a shop window. Her eyes sparkled with anticipation, as if that small object held all the magic in the world.

And just like that, my heart clenched. Pari.

Memories of her flooded my mind, uninvited but vivid, as if they had been waiting for the right moment to resurface. I could almost hear her laughter, feel the warmth of her presence beside me.

We used to play a game. *What Will Be I?* She would throw me a question, and I had to answer. *What will I be if I were a fruit? What will I be if I were an animal?* I still remember the day she asked me that last one.

"If you were an animal..." I had paused, pretending to think, enjoying the way she leaned forward, eager for my answer. "You'd be a unicorn."

Her face had lit up like a festival of lights. "A unicorn?" she repeated, her voice tinged with childlike wonder. "That's my favourite animal! Since I was little!" She had been so happy, so effortlessly joyful, and at that moment, I had wished I could give her the entire universe if it meant keeping that smile on her face forever.

But forever never lasts, does it?

Now, standing on this busy street, watching a stranger's daughter clutch at her father's hand, I felt an ache I hadn't let myself acknowledge in a long time. Time had moved on, the world had continued spinning, but some things remained. Some people remained etched into our hearts, woven into the smallest, most unexpected moments.

As I stood there, I kept glancing at the little girl's father, wondering if he would buy her the keychain, she had set her heart on. I could see the hesitation in his eyes, not because he didn't want to get it for her, but because something was in the way.

He turned to the vendor. "Do you accept online payments?"

The vendor shook his head. "Only cash."

Without hesitation, the father pulled out a ₹500 note, but once again, the vendor refused. "I don't have change," he said, shrugging.

I watched as the little girl's excitement slowly crumbled into disappointment. Her tiny hands, which had been eagerly reaching out just moments ago, now fell to her sides. Her hopeful expression faded, replaced by the unmistakable sadness of a child denied something they truly loved.

Something inside me stirred. A feeling I couldn't quite explain, or maybe one I knew too well.

I instinctively checked my wallet, there tucked between a few old receipts, was a    ₹50 note. Without a second thought, I stepped forward, handed it to the vendor, and took the keychain.

I knelt down and placed it gently in the little girl's palm.

Her eyes widened in surprise, and then, just like magic, her face lit up again. The disappointment vanished, replaced by unfiltered joy. She giggled, hugging the tiny unicorn charm as if it were the most precious thing in the world.

And in that moment, I was no longer in the present.

I was back in time, watching Pari smile in the very same way. The way her lips curled, the way her eyes sparkled like the stars, the way her laughter rang in the air, it was all the same. For a second, it felt like she was right there, that if I just reached out, I could touch that memory, hold onto it before it faded away again.

The little girl looked up at me and said, "Thank you."

I smiled, brushing a hand over her soft curls. "You're welcome."

Her father, touched by the gesture, insisted on paying me back. "I can send you the money online please, let me."

But I shook my head. "Her smile made my day. If anything, I should be the one thanking you."

He nodded, understanding. With a grateful look, he took his daughter's hand, and they walked away.

I stood there, watching them leave, feeling a strange mix of warmth and longing. Just before they disappeared into the crowd, the little girl turned back toward me. She smiled once more and waved.

I waved back, holding onto that moment, letting it settle deep inside me.

Some smiles stay with you forever.

And today, I had found another.

That day, I realized something being with Pari didn't mean I had to be by her side. She was everywhere. In the laughter of a child, in the melody of birds singing at dawn, in the fleeting joy of a stranger's smile. She had become a part of the world around me, woven into the fabric of my everyday life.

I had spent so much time believing that love meant presence, that to hold on to someone, you had to physically have them beside you. But life has a way of teaching lessons in the most unexpected moments. Pari wasn't just a person I had once known, she had become a feeling, an essence, a whisper in the wind, a warmth in the sunlight. I saw her in the little things: the soft rustling of leaves, the colours of the evening sky, the way the first drops of rain kissed the earth.

**They say time heals. But does it?**

Time doesn't erase the pain; it doesn't make you forget. It simply teaches you how to carry it, how to weave it into your being until it no longer feels like a wound but a part of who you are. Some losses are never meant to be forgotten. Some people are never meant to fade. And Pari, she wasn't just a memory. She was a part of me, living in every moment I chose to see her.

And so, I learned to live with it. Not by letting go, but by holding on differently.

I know now, Pari *did* have feelings for me once. Maybe not forever, maybe not as deeply as I had for her, but at some point in time, I mattered to her. There was a time when she looked at me with warmth, when my presence brought a smile to her face, when I was someone special to her. But that time has passed. Those feelings, whatever they were, have faded for her.

And that's okay.

Because for me, knowing that she once cared, that she once saw me the way I saw her that is enough. Enough to carry with me for a lifetime. Love doesn't always have to last forever to be real. It doesn't have to end with a happily ever after to be meaningful. Sometimes, love is just a fleeting moment, a brief chapter in our story that leaves a lasting imprint on our hearts.

Now, she is living her life, happy, moving forward without me. And strangely, that's exactly what I always wished for. Every prayer I ever whispered, every silent hope I held close, was never about making her stay, it was about making sure she was happy. That's all I ever wanted. And she *is* happy. The only difference is... she's happy without me.

That's it. That's the reality I've come to accept.

**And I've realized something, real love isn't about possession; it isn't about holding on when the other person is ready to let go. Sometimes, love means stepping back, watching from afar, and being content in knowing that the person you cherish is safe, smiling, and at peace.**

Even if that peace no longer includes me.

And maybe... that's its own kind of love too.

*Maybe the butterflies we chase aren't meant to be caught. Maybe they're meant to show us the beauty of letting go, watching their majestic colours shimmer in the light as they take flight, free and unbound. Perhaps love is the same. It was never about possession; it was always about appreciation, about cherishing something even when it was never ours to keep.*

We made just one mistake that's it. We fell in love, but we forgot to hold on to it. Maybe we assumed love was enough, that it could sustain itself without effort, without reassurance, without the quiet, unspoken promises to never let go. And before we knew it, it slipped through our fingers like grains of sand, like a butterfly that was never meant to stay.

But so, what if she isn't with me anymore? So, what if she has moved on, and I am nothing more than a passing memory in her story? That doesn't change how I feel. I still love her the same way I always did, not because I haven't found someone else, not because I'm trapped in the past, but because my heart never had time for anything else besides loving her.

Some loves don't fade. Some loves don't seek replacements.

And maybe, just maybe, that's okay.

I even asked her if we could start over. I told her, *Let's be strangers again. Let's erase the past, rewrite our story, and give it another chance.* Maybe, just maybe, we could find our way back to each other.

But she wasn't interested.

She had already moved on, already closed the chapter where my name was written. And that's when I understood sometimes, no matter how much you want to go back, the past remains the past. Some things aren't meant to be rewritten.

Maybe *forever* is just meant for memories, not people. Maybe we aren't supposed to hold on to anyone forever, just the moments, the love we once shared, the echoes of laughter that still linger in the corners of our minds.

All I ever wanted was to be loved the way I loved her. To be looked at the way I looked at her. But that's not possible now.

And maybe... it never was.

Even after everything, I still missed her like hell. No matter how much I tried to accept reality, there was this ache inside me, this emptiness that refused to fade. I felt incomplete, like a puzzle with a missing piece, like a melody that ended before its final note.

I started to believe I was just wasting my days, drowning in memories that no longer belonged to me. So, I decided to change. I thought if I kept myself busy, so busy that I had no time to think about her, maybe I'd be fine. Maybe the emptiness would disappear.

I tightened my schedule, filling every gap with something new. I joined a flute class, hoping to lose myself in the music, to create something beautiful out of the silence she left behind. I started taking better care of myself, fixing the things I had once neglected. I joined the gym, pushed my limits, and exhausted my body, thinking that if I was too tired to feel, maybe I wouldn't miss her so much.

From morning till night, I had no breaks, no moments of stillness. My day started at 6 AM and ended at 9 PM, packed with tasks, distractions, anything that could keep my mind from wandering back to her.

But no matter how much I tried, the feeling never left. Even with all the noise, I could still hear the silence she had left behind. Even with all the movement, I still felt stuck in the past.

And then, I realized the emptiness I was trying to fill wasn't just a feeling.

It was *her.*

No amount of distractions, no number of new hobbies, no rigid schedule could change that. Because sometimes, missing someone isn't just a thought you can push away, it's a part of you, a space in your heart that only they ever filled.

And no matter how much I tried to move forward, Pari was still the piece I couldn't replace.

Once, when Pari and I were in a relationship, she asked me about the NCC camp, the place where I saw her but never really spoke to her. But unlike what she had assumed, I *did* know her before the camp. I had been in love with her even then, but she had no idea. She was just living her life, unaware that someone in the same camp was silently admiring her, carrying a love too heavy to put into words.

She looked at me with curiosity. *"You saw me there, but you never spoke to me?"*

I nodded, a bittersweet smile tugging at my lips.

*"But why? Why did you act like that?"* she asked, tilting her head slightly.

I took a deep breath, searching for the right words. *"Because I was in love with you, Pari. And you had no idea."*

She frowned. *"But I talked to you, didn't I? On the last day, I came to you myself. And still… you just said 'bye' and left. You didn't even let the conversation finish."*

I looked down, my fingers tracing invisible patterns on the table. The memory of that moment still stung.

*"I know,"* I admitted, my voice barely above a whisper. *"And I regret it more than anything."*

Pari's gaze softened, but there was still confusion in her eyes. *"Why, Partha? Why did you do that?"*

I sighed, leaning back. *"Because I was scared. I was loving you so much, but I didn't know how to face you. I didn't know how to talk to you without my feelings getting in the way. And when you actually came to me, I panicked. I thought if I stayed, if I let the conversation go on, you'd see right through me."*

She shook her head, letting out a small sigh. *"How did you spend those ten days?"* she asked. *"Knowing that the person you loved was right there, but you still couldn't talk to her?"*

I let out a small, broken laugh. *"It was horrible,"* I admitted. *"Every single day, I wanted to talk to you. To just sit beside you, to hear your voice, to be a part of your world, even if only for a moment. But I was too much of a coward to admit it."*

I looked away for a second, lost in the memory of that camp, the stolen glances, the unspoken words, the ache of knowing she was so close yet so far.

*"And you know what?"* I added after a pause. *"It still hurts. Even now. Because those were the most painful ten days of my life."*

Pari didn't say anything for a moment. Maybe she was trying to understand what it must have felt like to love in silence, to carry something so heavy alone. Or maybe she realized that sometimes, the worst pain isn't rejection.

It's never even getting the chance to try.

That day, after hearing everything I had been through at the camp, how I spent ten days in silent agony, how I had loved her from afar but never found the courage to speak. Pari looked at me with something I hadn't seen before. A softness, an understanding, and something even deeper... love.

And then she made a promise.

*"No matter what happens, I won't leave you."*

Her words felt like a lifeline, like something I could hold on to forever. In that moment, I believed her. I believed that this love, *our* love, was strong enough to survive anything.

But promises, like people, change with time.

That promise has long since been broken. The words that once felt unshakable are now just echoes of the past. She *did* love me once,of that, I am sure. But not anymore. Not in the way she used to, not in the way I still love her.

And I do. I still love her.

They say some chapters in life are meant to be just memories. That no matter how much you wish to keep reading, you have to close the book and move forward. And maybe they're right.

So, I will fold the pages of the chapter where Pari was with me. I will keep them safe, tucked away in the corners of my heart, because even though she didn't make it to the end of my story.

She will always be my favourite chapter.

When we came together, we wrote a story, one filled with love, laughter, and moments that felt like forever. But when we parted, that story didn't just end. Instead, it split into three.

One was the story *you* understood,the one where things unfolded in a way that made sense to you, where you saw the reasons, the justifications, and the choices that led us here.

The second was the story *I* understood,the one that lived in my heart, where love was never the problem, only the silence between us. The version where I held on, even when you let go.

And then there was the third,the *unsaid* story.

The one we could have understood *together* if only we had talked. If only we had been honest about our fears, our doubts, our love. If only we had tried to fix what was breaking instead of walking away from it.

But we didn't.

And so, that third story remains unwritten, forever lost between what was and what could have been.

They say loving someone you cannot have is a weakness that it's foolish, that it's a waste of time, that it only leads to pain.

But I don't see it that way.

For me, it's the most *courageous* and *impartial* thing a person can do. To love without expecting anything in return, to care without conditions, to give without asking it takes strength. It takes resilience.

Because real love isn't about possession. It's not about demanding a place in someone's life. It's about wanting their happiness, even if it means watching from a distance. It's about carrying love in your heart, even when you know it has nowhere to go.

And if that's weakness, then I don't want to be strong.

It had been two months since our breakup.

I was sitting in the balcony, sipping coffee, my phone resting on the table beside me. Outside, the rain poured relentlessly, washing over the city, filling the air with that familiar earthy scent. I wasn't thinking about anything in particular just watching the raindrops race down the railing, lost in their quiet, unpredictable paths.

Then my phone rang.

At first, I thought of ignoring it. I wasn't in the mood for conversations, for interruptions. But for some reason one I couldn't quite understand. I turned my phone over to check who was calling.

And then I froze.

It was *Pari.*

My body tensed. My hands trembled slightly as I stared at the screen, my heart pounding so loudly I could feel it in my ears. My breath hitched, and before I could even process what was happening, my vision blurred.

I hadn't heard from her in two months. Two months of silence, of trying to move on, of convincing myself that she was just a memory now. And yet, here she was,her name glowing on my screen like a ghost from the past.

The call was about to end. If I hesitated even a second longer, it would go to voicemail.

So, I picked up.

*"Hello?"* her voice came through, soft yet uncertain.

The moment I heard her, something inside me cracked. My eyes burned, my throat tightened, and for a second, I felt like I couldn't breathe. It was ridiculous how a single word from her could unravel everything I had spent weeks trying to hold together.

But I swallowed the lump in my throat, forced myself to steady my voice, and replied,

*"Hello."*

*"How are you?"* Pari asked, her voice hesitant, almost unsure.

*"I'm fine... and you?"* I replied, trying to sound indifferent, though my heart was anything but calm.

*"I'm fine too,"* she said.

*"Okay."*

And then,silence.

A long, awkward, suffocating silence.

I could hear the faint sound of rain outside, the distant hum of the city, the rhythmic ticking of the clock on the wall. But between us, there was nothing. Just a hollow emptiness where words used to be.

I remembered the days when we would fight to talk to each other, when words flowed effortlessly between us, when time didn't matter because there was always something more to say. We would talk for hours, never running out of stories, of thoughts, of dreams.

And now? After just fifteen seconds, we had nothing.

Not that I *really* had nothing to say. If anything, I had *too much*, so many questions, so many things I wanted to ask. *Why did you call? Do you miss me? Do you ever think about us? Are you happy without me?*

But I knew better.

Some questions don't bring closure, they only open old wounds. And I wasn't sure if either of us was ready for that.

So, I stayed quiet, swallowing everything I wanted to say.

Because sometimes, silence speaks louder than words ever could.

Then, Pari spoke, breaking the silence between us.

*"What are you doing?"* she asked, her voice soft, almost hesitant.

I took a deep breath, gripping my coffee mug a little tighter. *"I was just having my evening coffee,"* I replied, trying to sound casual, as if this call wasn't shaking me to my core.

But then I noticed it,*my voice was giving up.*

No matter how much I tried to control it, to sound normal, the cracks were there. My voice trembled, betraying me, exposing the storm I was holding back. It was the weight of everything I had suppressed the emotions, the questions, the memories all pressing against my throat, begging to be let out.

I bit my lip, forcing myself to stay composed. *Not now. Don't break now.*

But the tears were there, sitting in the corners of my eyes, threatening to fall. I could feel the ache in my chest, the struggle to breathe through the weight of unspoken words.

And yet, I kept my voice steady. I had to.

Because the last thing I wanted was for her to hear just how much I was still hurting.

With a strong heart and a voice I barely recognized as my own, I finally asked the question that had been burning inside me since the moment I saw her name on my screen.

*"Why did you call me, Pari?"*

She took a breath, the kind that made me feel like she was choosing her words carefully.

*"No... I just felt like talking to you,"* she replied, her voice calm, almost distant.

*"Oh... is that so?"* I said, my tone neutral, though inside, a storm was raging.

For a second, I let myself believe,believe that maybe, just maybe, she had missed me. That maybe there was a small part of her that still cared. But before that thought could settle, she spoke again.

*"Don't get your hopes up,"* she said firmly, as if she could read my mind. *"I just wanted to talk to you, that's it. There's nothing else."*

And just like that, whatever flicker of hope had appeared inside me was gone.

I swallowed hard, forcing myself to smile bitterly as I looked out at the rain. Of course. I should have known. This wasn't some grand gesture, some sign that she still felt something. It was just a moment of impulse for her, something temporary. Something that meant nothing.

But to me?

It meant *everything.*

I smiled, though it hurt more than I could ever put into words.

*"I know, Maa,"* I said, my voice calm, steady, even though my heart was anything but. *"I was the one who made all the mistakes. Why would you come back, right?"*

I let out a soft chuckle, one of those hollow laughs that hide more pain than they reveal.

*"But I'm really okay. I'm feeling good. Not because I've stopped loving you. Because that will never happen. I will always love you, Pari. You were, are, and always will be the only love of my life. There was no one before you, and there will be no one after you."*

I paused for a moment, letting my words settle between us. There was no expectation in them, no hidden plea. Just the truth.

*"I won't force you to give me another chance. I know that's not what you want. I just want you to be happy, that's all I've ever wanted."*

I took a deep breath, steadying myself before continuing.

*"But just know... I'm still here. If you ever need anything, anytime, I'll be there. Even though you've blocked me from everywhere, it doesn't change a thing for me."*

I swallowed the lump in my throat. *"I still care, Pari."*

And with that, I let the silence return. Only this time, it wasn't awkward. It was filled with all the things left unsaid, all the feelings that would never truly fade.

*"Not as your partner,"* I continued, my voice softer now. *"I'll be there as your friend too, if that's what you need. I know it's hard, but if that's what you want, I'll make it possible."*

There was a pause. I could hear Pari take a deep breath on the other end before she finally spoke.

*"I just called to tell you... to move on from our relationship."*

Her words felt like a blade, sharp and precise, cutting through whatever little hope I had left.

I closed my eyes for a moment, letting the weight of it settle inside me. I knew this was coming. Maybe I had always known. But knowing didn't make it hurt any less.

*"That will never happen, Pari maa,"* I said, calling her by the name I once used with so much love. *"I truly love you. You have a permanent place in my heart."*

I exhaled slowly, steadying my voice before continuing.

*"If that's all you called for, then I'll hang up. I won't give you any trouble. I won't even show my face to you. I'll love you from a distance, that's something my heart has decided, and you can't control that."*

There was silence. A silence that spoke of finality, of things that could never be changed.

*"If there's ever anything else... if you ever need to talk... call me. I will always keep my promise. I'll be there for you, for every problem, no matter what."*

I swallowed the lump in my throat, took one last breath, and said the hardest words of all.

*"Goodbye, Pari."*

And before she could say anything else, before I could second-guess myself, I hung up.

The call ended, but the ache in my chest remained.

When we came together, we wrote a story, one filled with love, laughter, and moments that felt like forever. But when we parted, that story didn't just end. Instead, it split into three.

One was the story *you* understood,the one where things unfolded in a way that made sense to you, where you saw the reasons, the justifications, and the choices that led us here.

The second was the story *I* understood,the one that lived in my heart, where love was never the problem, only the silence between us. The version where I held on, even when you let go.

And then there was the third,the *unsaid* story.

The one we could have understood *together* if only we had talked. If only we had been honest about our fears, our doubts, our love. If only we had tried to fix what was breaking instead of walking away from it.

But we didn't.

And so, that third story remains unwritten, forever lost between what was and what could have been.

They say loving someone you cannot have is a weakness that it's foolish, that it's a waste of time, that it only leads to pain.

But I don't see it that way.

For me, it's the most *courageous* and *impartial* thing a person can do. To love without expecting anything in return, to care without conditions, to give without asking it takes strength. It takes resilience.

Because real love isn't about possession. It's not about demanding a place in someone's life. It's about wanting their happiness, even if it means watching from a distance. It's about carrying love in your heart, even when you know it has nowhere to go.

And if that's weakness, then I don't want to be strong.

It had been two months since our breakup.

I was sitting in the balcony, sipping coffee, my phone resting on the table beside me. Outside, the rain poured relentlessly, washing over the city, filling the air with that familiar earthy scent. I wasn't thinking about anything in particular just watching the raindrops race down the railing, lost in their quiet, unpredictable paths.

Then my phone rang.

At first, I thought of ignoring it. I wasn't in the mood for conversations, for interruptions. But for some reason one I couldn't quite understand. I turned my phone over to check who was calling.

And then I froze.

It was *Pari.*

My body tensed. My hands trembled slightly as I stared at the screen, my heart pounding so loudly I could feel it in my ears. My breath hitched, and before I could even process what was happening, my vision blurred.

I hadn't heard from her in two months. Two months of silence, of trying to move on, of convincing myself that she was just a memory now. And yet, here she was,her name glowing on my screen like a ghost from the past.

The call was about to end. If I hesitated even a second longer, it would go to voicemail.

So, I picked up.

*"Hello?"* her voice came through, soft yet uncertain.

The moment I heard her, something inside me cracked. My eyes burned, my throat tightened, and for a second, I felt like I couldn't breathe. It was ridiculous how a single word from her could unravel everything I had spent weeks trying to hold together.

But I swallowed the lump in my throat, forced myself to steady my voice, and replied,

*"Hello."*

*"How are you?"* Pari asked, her voice hesitant, almost unsure.

*"I'm fine... and you?"* I replied, trying to sound indifferent, though my heart was anything but calm.

*"I'm fine too,"* she said.

*"Okay."*

And then, silence.

A long, awkward, suffocating silence.

I could hear the faint sound of rain outside, the distant hum of the city, the rhythmic ticking of the clock on the wall. But between us, there was nothing. Just a hollow emptiness where words used to be.

I remembered the days when we would fight to talk to each other, when words flowed effortlessly between us, when time didn't matter because there was always something more to say. We would talk for hours, never running out of stories, of thoughts, of dreams.

And now? After just fifteen seconds, we had nothing.

Not that I *really* had nothing to say. If anything, I had *too much*, so many questions, so many things I wanted to ask. *Why did you call? Do you miss me? Do you ever think about us?*

*Are you happy without me?*

But I knew better.

Some questions don't bring closure, they only open old wounds. And I wasn't sure if either of us was ready for that. So, I stayed quiet, swallowing everything I wanted to say.

Because sometimes, silence speaks louder than words ever could.

Then, Pari spoke, breaking the silence between us.

*"What are you doing?"* she asked, her voice soft, almost hesitant.

I took a deep breath, gripping my coffee mug a little tighter. *"I was just having my evening coffee,"* I replied, trying to sound casual, as if this call wasn't shaking me to my core.

But then I noticed it,*my voice was giving up.*

No matter how much I tried to control it, to sound normal, the cracks were there. My voice trembled, betraying me, exposing the storm I was holding back. It was the weight of everything I had suppressed the emotions, the questions, the memories all pressing against my throat, begging to be let out.

I bit my lip, forcing myself to stay composed. *Not now. Don't break now.*

But the tears were there, sitting in the corners of my eyes, threatening to fall. I could feel the ache in my chest, the struggle to breathe through the weight of unspoken words.

And yet, I kept my voice steady. I had to.

Because the last thing I wanted was for her to hear just how much I was still hurting.

With a strong heart and a voice I barely recognized as my own, I finally asked the question that had been burning inside me since the moment I saw her name on my screen.

*"Why did you call me, Pari?"*

She took a breath, the kind that made me feel like she was choosing her words carefully.

*"No... I just felt like talking to you,"* she replied, her voice calm, almost distant.

*"Oh... is that so?"* I said, my tone neutral, though inside, a storm was raging.

For a second, I let myself believe, believe that maybe, just maybe, she had missed me. That maybe there was a small part of her that still cared. But before that thought could settle, she spoke again.

*"Don't get your hopes up,"* she said firmly, as if she could read my mind. *"I just wanted to talk to you, that's it. There's nothing else."*

And just like that, whatever flicker of hope had appeared inside me was gone.

I swallowed hard, forcing myself to smile bitterly as I looked out at the rain. Of course. I should have known. This wasn't some grand gesture, some sign that she still felt something. It was just a moment of impulse for her, something temporary. Something that meant nothing.

But to me?

It meant *everything.*

I smiled, though it hurt more than I could ever put into words.

*"I know, Maa,"* I said, my voice calm, steady, even though my heart was anything but. *"I was the one who made all the mistakes. Why would you come back, right?"*

I let out a soft chuckle, one of those hollow laughs that hide more pain than they reveal.

*"But I'm really okay. I'm feeling good. Not because I've stopped loving you. Because that will never happen. I will always love you, Pari. You were, are, and always will be the only love of my life. There was no one before you, and there will be no*

*one after you."*

I paused for a moment, letting my words settle between us. There was no expectation in them, no hidden plea. Just the truth.

*"I won't force you to give me another chance. I know that's not what you want. I just want you to be happy, that's all I've ever wanted."*

I took a deep breath, steadying myself before continuing.

*"But just know... I'm still here. If you ever need anything, anytime, I'll be there. Even though you've blocked me from everywhere, it doesn't change a thing for me."*

I swallowed the lump in my throat. *"I still care, Pari."*

And with that, I let the silence return. Only this time, it wasn't awkward. It was filled with all the things left unsaid, all the feelings that would never truly fade.

*"Not as your partner,"* I continued, my voice softer now. *"I'll be there as your friend too, if that's what you need. I know it's hard, but if that's what you want, I'll make it possible."*

There was a pause. I could hear Pari take a deep breath on the other end before she finally spoke.

*"I just called to tell you... to move on from our relationship."*

Her words felt like a blade, sharp and precise, cutting through whatever little hope I had left.

I closed my eyes for a moment, letting the weight of it settle inside me. I knew this was coming. Maybe I had always known. But knowing didn't make it hurt any less.

*"That will never happen, Pari maa,"* I said, calling her by the name I once used with so much love. *"I truly love you. You have a permanent place in my heart."*

I exhaled slowly, steadying my voice before continuing.

*"If that's all you called for, then I'll hang up. I won't give you any trouble. I won't even show my face to you. I'll love you*

*from a distance, that's something my heart has decided, and you can't control that."*

There was silence. A silence that spoke of finality, of things that could never be changed.

*"If there's ever anything else... if you ever need to talk... call me. I will always keep my promise. I'll be there for you, for every problem, no matter what."*

I swallowed the lump in my throat, took one last breath, and said the hardest words of all.

*"Goodbye, Pari."*

And before she could say anything else, before I could second-guess myself, I hung up.

The call ended, but the ache in my chest remained.

After that call, I felt like I couldn't breathe. My chest felt heavy, my mind restless. I needed air,*something* to clear my thoughts before they drowned me completely.

So, I grabbed my umbrella and stepped outside.

The rain was still falling, but not as heavily as before. It was softer now, a mist-like drizzle that coated the streets in a thin, shimmering layer. The air was cold, crisp, carrying the scent of wet earth and something nostalgic something that reminded me of old conversations, of late-night walks, of moments I once thought would last forever.

I pulled my hood over my head, tucked my hands into my pockets, and started walking.

The streets were quieter than usual, the world seemingly wrapped in a peaceful haze. Streetlights flickered against the wet pavement, their reflections stretching and bending like something out of a dream. With each step, I tried to focus on the sound of my own footsteps, the rhythmic patter of the rain, anything but the lingering echo of *her* voice in my head.

But it was impossible.

Everywhere I looked, I saw something that reminded me of Pari. The way the raindrops clung to the leaves, just like they did that evening we got caught in the rain together. The way a passing couple laughed under a shared umbrella, lost in their own little world. The faint scent of coffee from a nearby shop, reminding me of the countless cups we once shared, of conversations that never seemed to end.

I let out a shaky breath.

No matter how much I tried to escape it, she was *everywhere.* In the rain. In the cold breeze. In the silence between my own thoughts.

Maybe that's just how love works. You don't always get to keep it, but it stays with you,woven into the smallest moments, hidden in the corners of your world, waiting to be remembered.

As I kept walking, lost in my thoughts, I suddenly spotted a familiar face.

Sitting on the stairs of a building complex, sheltering himself from the rain, was the homeless wanderer. His unkempt hair was damp, his old clothes clinging to his thin frame, and in his hands, he rummaged through a big plastic bag as if searching for something important.

I had known him for around four years, ever since I first shifted to this city.

I remembered our first encounter vividly. One evening, he had approached me, not to beg for money, but to ask for food. I had reached into my pockets, only to realize I had nothing to offer. The only thing I had was money, so I handed him a few notes. But to my surprise, he refused.

*"I don't want money,"* he had said, his voice low yet firm. *"If you don't mind, can you buy me some food instead? They won't let me inside the restaurant nearby because of how I look."*

His words had struck something deep within me.

Back then, I had just moved to the city, full of my own struggles, my own worries, and yet, in that moment, I felt a different kind of helplessness, the kind that comes from seeing someone who just wanted something as simple as a meal but had to rely on the kindness of strangers for it.

So, without hesitation, I had gone inside the restaurant and bought him a hot meal.

I still remembered the way his tired eyes had lit up, the gratitude in his voice as he thanked me over and over.

And now, years later, here he was again, sitting in the same city, in the same rain. Something about that felt... strange. Maybe because so much in my life had changed, and yet, here he was unchanged, unmoved by time, as if the world had simply forgotten about him.

I stood there for a moment, watching him, wondering if he would recognize me after all these years.

I remembered that day clearly the day I bought him food.

As he sat there eating, he looked at me and asked, *"What are you studying?"* His question took me by surprise. It was rare to see a homeless man speak with such awareness, such curiosity.

I told him about my degree, and he nodded, asking me a few more things,things that made me realize he wasn't an ordinary wanderer. There was a sharpness in his mind, a depth in his words that didn't quite match his current state.

Curious, I finally asked him, *"What made you choose this life? Why do you roam like this?"*

He didn't answer immediately. For a few seconds, he just stared at the rain, his fingers absentmindedly picking at the plastic bag he carried. Then, in a voice heavy with something I couldn't quite place, he said,

*"I lost my wife to cancer."*

A lump formed in my throat.

*"I spent everything I had to save her. Every last penny. But in the end, it didn't matter. She was gone."*

And suddenly, everything made sense. The sadness in his eyes, the way he wandered without purpose, the slight instability in his mind. It wasn't just homelessness,it was grief. Grief that had shattered him beyond repair.

That day, as I was about to leave, I heard him cry out, his voice raw and filled with rage.

*"What did I ask from God? A heaven? No! I just asked Him to save my wife. She was rightfully mine! I had earned her with all my love. But He took her away from me!"*

I had stood there, frozen, watching him curse the sky, curse fate, curse a God who had ignored his prayers.

That was the day I realized, love isn't just about feeling something; it's about *acting* before it's too late.

That was the day I decided I couldn't waste any more time. I had to tell Pari how I felt.

Because destiny... destiny is cruel to some people. And I wasn't going to let it be cruel to me.

That day, when I saw him cursing God, I didn't truly understand the depth of his pain.

I had assumed it was because of his mental instability, that maybe his mind had shattered under the weight of his suffering. But today, as I replayed that scene in my head, as I stood in the middle of the rain, feeling the hollowness inside me, I finally understood.

His rage, his words, his desperation none of it came from madness. It came from *loss.*

The kind of loss that makes you question everything you once believed in. The kind of loss that leaves you screaming into the void, demanding answers that will never come.

The cursing of God wasn't a sign of his instability, it was a cry from a heart that had been broken beyond repair. It was the pain of losing someone who meant *everything* to him.

And now, I knew exactly how that felt.

Seeing him sitting there in the cold, shivering slightly as the misty rain continued to fall, something in me stirred. Without thinking twice, I turned and walked into a nearby coffee shop.

The warmth of the café wrapped around me as I stepped inside, the aroma of freshly brewed coffee filling the air. I ordered two cups, one for me and one for him. As I waited, I found myself lost in memories again, of that first encounter, of the things he had told me, of how I had dismissed his pain as part of his instability. But now, I knew better.

With two steaming cups in my hands, I walked back to where he sat.

Approaching him, I held out a cup. *"Here,"* I said, my voice calm yet firm.

He looked up at me, his tired eyes scanning my face. I could tell he didn't recognize me, it had been four years, after all. Time had changed me, just as it had changed him.

For a moment, he hesitated, then slowly reached out and took the coffee from my hands.

I didn't say anything else. I just stood there, watching him take the first sip. His fingers wrapped tightly around the warm cup, his expression softening as the heat spread through him.

There was something oddly peaceful about that moment. two strangers standing together in the rain, bound by nothing but the silent understanding of loss, of time, of unspoken pain.

I sipped my own coffee, staring at the street ahead, letting the quiet settle between us. Sometimes, words weren't needed. Sometimes, just sharing a warm cup of coffee on a rainy evening was enough.

Then, after a few moments of silence, I asked him, *"How are you?"*

He looked at me briefly before replying, *"I'm fine."* His voice was calm, but there was a tiredness in it, like someone who had long stopped expecting anything from the world.

I nodded, not wanting to push the conversation further. He took another sip of coffee, then set the cup down beside him and started rummaging through his large plastic bag, his fingers searching for something.

After a while, he finally pulled out a book, a worn-out, tattered notebook with pages that looked like they had survived years of use. He placed it carefully on his lap, as if it held something precious, and went back to drinking his coffee.

I watched him, wondering what was in that book. Was it something important? A memory? A remnant of his past life? But I didn't ask. I figured it was just a habit, something he did regularly, a part of his routine.

But then, after finishing his coffee, he picked up the book again, flipped through a few pages, and started writing.

Curiosity got the better of me.

*"What are you writing?"* I asked, leaning slightly to get a glimpse.

He didn't answer. He just kept writing, as if he hadn't heard me at all.

I waited for a response, but none came. Realizing that he probably didn't want to share, I decided not to ask again. Some things were personal, and maybe this was one of those things.

So, I just sat there beside him, listening to the sound of raindrops hitting the pavement, watching the city move around us, and wondering what kind of stories were hidden inside that old notebook.

Suddenly, he stopped writing and, without looking at me, handed me the book.

*"It's my wife,"* he said, his voice quiet but steady.

I furrowed my brows, confused. At first, I thought maybe he was just saying something incoherent, a result of his unstable state. But as I hesitated, looking down at the worn-out book in my hands, curiosity got the better of me, and I opened it.

The pages were filled with handwritten notes, scribbled thoughts, and daily events, as if he was explaining his life to someone. The ink had faded in some places, and the handwriting was uneven, but the words carried a strange sense of warmth, like a conversation between two people who deeply knew each other.

As I flipped through the pages, it became clear, he was writing everything down for his wife.

*"I write everything I do here,"* he said, his eyes distant, as if he was seeing someone I couldn't. *"So my wife can read it."*

His words hit me in a way I hadn't expected.

I continued scanning through the pages, but his handwriting was a little hard to read, so I could only pick up bits and pieces a memory, a walk, a cup of tea, the way the sky looked on a certain evening. He described his days to her as if she were still there, as if she was just waiting for him to come home and tell her everything.

I felt a lump forming in my throat.

There was something both beautiful and heartbreaking about it. He wasn't just surviving he was holding on to his love, refusing to let time erase it. Maybe writing in that book made him feel like she was still with him, listening, smiling, responding in the way he remembered.

I didn't say anything.

After a few more moments, I closed the book gently and handed it back to him. He took it carefully, like it was the most precious thing in the world, and held it close.

I didn't need to read everything in that book to understand its significance.

Love doesn't always need a presence. Sometimes, just the belief that someone is still listening even if only in our hearts is enough to keep us going.

That was the moment I realized even I could do the same.

I had spent every waking moment lost in thoughts of Pari, trying to silence the ache that refused to fade. I had kept myself busy, filled my days with routines and distractions, but nothing had worked. No matter how much I tried, she lingered in my heart like an unfinished melody, a love song stuck on repeat.

But maybe... maybe I didn't have to *get over her*. Maybe I didn't need to erase her presence or force myself to forget.

Maybe, like this man, I could find my own way of healing.

I could write.

I could pour out everything I had left unsaid, the words I never had the courage to speak, the thoughts that haunted me, the memories that made my heart ache and swell at the same time. I could tell her about my day, about the little things I noticed, about how much I missed her.

Not because I expected her to read it. Not because I hoped she would come back.

But because some love stories don't need an audience.

Some love stories exist just for the sake of love itself.

I took a deep breath, feeling something shift inside me, a quiet resolve settling where there had only been restlessness before. I knew it wouldn't be easy. I knew writing wouldn't magically take away the pain. But at least, it would give it a place to go.

And maybe, just maybe, it would help me find peace.

And then another thought crossed my mind, she had blocked me everywhere.

If I sent her a message, it would go through, but she wouldn't see it. It would just sit there, unread, unseen, existing in a space where only I knew about it.

And maybe... that was enough.

Maybe it wasn't about her seeing my words or responding to them. Maybe it was about me *saying* them, about finally letting them go instead of holding them inside, suffocating under their weight.

I could send her everything I never got to say. I could tell her about my day, about how much I missed her, about how certain places still reminded me of her, how certain songs still carried her laughter in their melody.

I wouldn't expect a reply. I wouldn't even wait for one.

But just knowing that my words had reached the place where she once existed in my life where we had built our love, where we had shared our dreams that would be enough.

Because love doesn't always need acknowledgment.

Sometimes, love is just having the courage to express it, even when there's no one left to listen.

I still remember that one day, I told Pari something on my birthday.

I had promised her something.

I had told her that one day, I would write a book about our love story. A book filled with every moment we had shared, every dream we had whispered to each other, every fight we had overcome, every smile that had made my heart race.

I even had a title for it,***REBLOOMED LOVE***.

And beneath it, a subtitle that held all the meaning in the world to me: *A love that never ended.*

Back then, I truly believed our story would last forever. I thought the book would stretch across a lifetime, its pages growing thicker with each passing year, with every anniversary, with every promise we kept. I imagined giving it to her on our 50th anniversary, watching her smile as she flipped through the chapters of *us*.

But now… that book didn't have more than three years' worth of chapters.

The story that was supposed to last a lifetime had been cut short.

The pages I had dreamed of filling had been left empty, blank spaces where our future should have been. The love story I thought would reach a million pages had stopped, suddenly and painfully, before I could even write its middle.

And yet, even though she was no longer in my life, even though our love had not lasted the way I hoped it would…

It still lived inside me.

Perhaps the book would never be finished the way I imagined, but still I wrote it.

Not as a story of two people who grew old together.

But as a story of a love that, no matter how much time passed, never truly ended.

It's been some time now since our breakup.

And yet, I still find myself texting her, even though I know she will never reply.

It's not about waiting for an answer. It's not about hoping she will come back. It's just… habit. A habit of sharing my thoughts with the one person who once meant the world to me.

I find her in everything I do.

In every tune of a song that plays softly in the background. In the laughter of a child that reminds me of her carefree giggles. In the rustling of leaves, whispering memories of our late-night walks.

I see her in the sky, when the moon shines bright, just like the way her eyes used to when she talked about things she loved. I see her in the morning, when clouds scatter across the sky, reminding me of the lazy Sundays we spent dreaming about the future.

She has become an inseparable part of me, woven into my very existence.

No force in this world, not time, not distance, not even Pari herself can take her away from me.

Because you can't unlove someone you truly loved.

Love isn't something you switch off like a light. It's something that lingers, that stays. It changes shape, it transforms, but it never truly disappears.

And maybe that's the hardest part.

Not losing her.

But learning to live with the love that still remains.

♡♡♡

Love has a strange way of staying with us, even when the person we once held close has long since walked away. It lingers in the smallest details of our lives, in the scent of rain on a quiet evening, in a song playing softly in the background, in the way the moonlight filters through the curtains at night. We may try to escape it, bury it beneath the rush of our daily routines, or convince ourselves that time will erase it. But love,true love does not fade. It transforms, taking on new shapes, settling into the deepest corners of our hearts, where it continues to live.

This story is not just about heartbreak, it is about the echoes of love that refuse to fade, about learning to carry love without being consumed by it. We often believe that love must last forever to be real, that it must have a happy ending to be meaningful. But sometimes, the truest love stories are the ones that remain unfinished. They are the ones that teach us the most, not about the person we loved, but about ourselves.

There was a time when I believed love was about holding on, about fighting against all odds to keep someone in my life. But now I know that love is also about letting go, about allowing someone to find their own happiness, even if it doesn't include you. It is about learning to love from a distance, to cherish memories without letting them chain you to the past.

I once promised to write a book about our love story, to fill its pages with every moment we shared. I imagined it stretching across a lifetime, a love that would endure every storm. But life had other plans. The story was shorter than I expected, its pages fewer than I had hoped. And yet, it was beautiful. Every word, every memory, every moment spent with her was worth it.

Maybe some love stories aren't meant to last a lifetime. Maybe they are meant to be remembered, to be cherished as a part of who we are. And maybe, just maybe, love doesn't need a perfect ending to be real.

Because love, in its purest form, never truly leaves us. It stays, not in the presence of the person we once loved, but in the way it shaped us, in the way it taught us to feel, to hope, to dream. And perhaps, that is enough.

ᗡᗡᗡ